I0549153

Lyndon Publishing

Airtight Case For Love

Janice Olson

Lyndon Publishing

Airtight Case For Love
Copyright © 2016 by Janice Olson

Requests for information should be addressed to:
Lyndon Publishing
2200 S. Smith Berry Rd., Suite 200
Pantego, Texas 76013
Website: www.LyndonPublishing.com

ISBN: **978-0-9885263-0-3**

For more information about Janice Olson, please access the author's Website at:
www.JaniceOlson.com, or email her at Janice at Janice Olson dot com

Cover image, original photograph manipulated by Harry Olson, all rights reserved.

Lyndon Publishing Mission Statement:

To the best of our ability, publish, and distribute inspirational products that offer exceptional value and Biblical encouragement to the world while honoring God.

Acknowledgement

To God be the glory, all things He has done.

God receives all the glory for this book. Without His hand
on my life, my books would not be written.
And thank you to my husband, Harry, who is always there.

Note from the Author:

When I had no thought of becoming an author, God created in
me the ability to write stories.

As a dyslexic author, I am often faced with challenges. The
process of thinking up and developing the stories is generally the
easy part of writing for me. The hardest of writing comes when I
try to bring order to the sometimes elusive and chaotic words
floating around in my brain, and then again when I transfer those
thoughts to my fingers onto the page.

With all the inevitable roadblocks dyslexia may cause, I enjoy
the journey. My books give my readers hours of good, clean
reading enjoyment, to which I hope you will agree. Writing also
gives me the pleasure of knowing I'm no longer that scared little
girl who read slowly, but comprehended little.

Join me as Seth Singleton and Lori Morgan begin a merry
chase of that sometimes-elusive thing called *Love*. Seth and
Lori's story of *happily ever after* first comes with setbacks,
misunderstandings, and a whole lot of fun.

Enjoy the ride.
Blessings,

Janice Olson

Your Dyslexic author

Mailing Address: Janice Olson, P.O. Box 382380, Duncanville, Texas 75132
Or you may Email: Janice at Janice Olson dot com

As I respect your time, please respect mine. No junk mail please.

5

Airtight Case For Love

"In vain have I struggled. It will not do. My feelings will not be repressed.
You must allow me to tell you how ardently I admire and love you."
Jane Austen - Pride and Prejudice

Chapter 1

Seth

"Hey, Princess, since you caught the bouquet and I caught the garter, does this mean our wedding will be next?"

Standing in the midst of the other bridesmaids, Lori Morgan's narrow-eyed stare wanted to impale me to the ground. Her pretty face turned an appealing shade of pink, setting off her snapping blue eyes and golden hair, as invisible steam poured from her ears.

"Seth Singleton."

My name was ground out through Lori's tightly clenched teeth. Smiling, I knew I had crawled under her skin and caused her a good deal of irritation.

The other girls in the group chuckled while flirting.

I winked at them. In return they giggled again, that is, all except Lori.

Lori's lips formed a straight line.

I saw a spark of that *get-even* look in her eyes.

"Why, Cowboy,"—she gave a sickly sweet smile—"I do believe your thinking's terribly flawed. I guess you haven't heard. You'd be the last man on earth I'd hook my star to." She cocked her brow. "And in case that isn't plain enough for you … I'd rather be an old maid spinster than to be married to the likes of you. In fact, in the future, if it seems I am going out of my way to avoid you—like now— you'd be correct in your thinking."

Baring her teeth, she flashed me a *drop-dead* look, before turning in the opposite direction and putting as much distance as she could between her and me. Her hips swayed while she held her nose high in the air like she smelled a stench of something dead—*me, no doubt*.

I gave her a two-finger salute to her back. "Touché, Princess, touché." I chuckled loudly, causing the other ladies in the group to giggle before following in Lori's direction, but not before one of them winked at me.

"You can call me anytime, Cowboy. I'd be more than happy to hook my star to yours." The woman smiled suggestively before walking away. Her hips swayed like there was no tomorrow.

I mumbled. "I'm afraid you'll wait a long time for that call, sweetheart." Shaking my head, I wondered how she kept her hips from getting out of joint.

Come to think of it, I shouldn't have embarrassed Lori like that in front of the other bridesmaids.

Somehow, after my run-ins with her at the children's Christmas play, and the few times during my sister's wedding rehearsal, I couldn't resist baiting her to see what she'd do or say next. It was becoming a game with me, one a grown man shouldn't play with such a desirable woman like Lori.

The racket of the tin cans rattling on the pavement had me heading to where the small crowd moved forward, waving off the happy couple as they drove away.

I pushed to the front line to watch them leave. Seeing my sister, Whitney, wag her finger at me from the car, smiling, was worth all the trouble I'd gone to—digging through the garage and tying the cans to the undercarriage. At least, it made my baby sister happy and gave her something more to remember about her wedding day.

Mr. and Mrs. Adam Ryder. Their happiness almost made me wish I had someone to go home to at night … but not quite. Not with my job.

A heavy sigh coming from one of the bridesmaids drew my attention. There she was, Lori, the object of my teasing. For some reason, I took pleasure in trying to throw her off kilter and make her temper boil.

Knowing she wouldn't be pleased to see me, I maneuvered myself over next to her.

"*Ahh*, there goes the happy couple."

Lori groused under her breath, something about me being a jerk.

I turned, looking down at her. "What? No tears? No weepy goodbyes? Not even a tissue to dab your eyes?" I shouldn't have taunted her, but I couldn't help myself. I nodded at the mothers and a couple of the bridesmaids wiping their eyes.

"I thought you would be crying like all the other women, especially since it was your brother who got married today."

She gave a snort of disgust. "You don't have an ounce of kindness in your blood. You're cold, unfeeling, and wouldn't know love if it smacked you in the face."

Her cute little mouth was drawn in a straight line again.

I'm bad. My sister, Whitney, will have my hide for provoking her new sister-in-law.

"In fact, I doubt you will ever get married with your rotten attitude because no one will have you." She gave me a look of "drop dead."

A smirk rode my lips. I wasn't about to let Lori know she had drawn and wielded the sharp edge of her tongue with precision and so perilously close to the quick. I wanted to extract a pound of flesh in retaliation.

"Darlin' if I wanted to get married, I could. But certainly not to someone who has her nose out of joint every time we meet."

She stomped her dainty little foot. "*Oooh*, you're impossible. Why don't you grow up?" She pounced her free hand on her thin waist, her other still held the bridal bouquet she'd caught.

"For your information, my nose isn't out of joint. In fact, up until I met you, I have never lost my temper so quickly or disliked someone as much as I do you. You're insufferable. Pigheaded. Coldhearted. You even like to terrorize children. You're—"

"Stop right there, lady." I used my strong, commanding Police Detective voice, the one used to gain criminals' attention. "I *don't* terrorize children. In fact, I love kids and kids love me. Just ask my niece Mandy. She'll tell you."

"I don't need to ask your niece. I saw you in action at the children's Christmas play two weeks ago. You scared little Tommy half to death with your threat to haul him off to jail and throw away the key. The little guy was in tears. He wouldn't go near you for the rest of the evening."

"At least, he started behaving, didn't he?" I let loose a chuckle to let her think she hadn't gotten under my skin. It was. For sure, the woman could give back as good as she got.

"And furthermore, I didn't see a single tear roll down Tommy's cheek. In fact, he allowed you to help him get dressed in his costume. Which I might add, you'd still be trying to coax him into that dress if I hadn't stepped in to help."

"It wasn't a dress. It was a shepherd's tunic. And I was doing just fine. I didn't need your help."

"Well, lady, the way it looked to me—"

"My name is Lori. L.O.R.I. Not lady. Not darlin'. Not princess, or any other derivative you might think to call me. Lori. See if you can remember that the next time we meet."

She squared her shoulders giving me the full blast of those beautiful eyes of hers.

"Better yet, my attitude would improve immensely if you would stay as far away from me as possible. So please do your best to remember that in the future."

Lori turned her stiff back to me once again before stomping off to where her mother and stepfather, Jim and Audrey Ryder, were talking to my parents, both couples happy in-laws of the newlyweds who'd just left on their honeymoon.

I couldn't tear my gaze from the fascinating sway of her hips. I had to remember to close my mouth to keep from drooling on my tux.

That woman could sure captivate my attention without even trying. It's a shame she was so acidic in nature. Otherwise, she might have made a good friend—emphasis on friend—to ask out to dinner or a movie from time to time. It was for sure, that gal was too caustic to ever be a love interest.

Her snub shouldn't have irritated me so, but it did. I ought to have been glad to see the back of her. She was nothing but a stuck up snob. Howbeit, a beautiful stuck up snob. One I hoped to have little interaction with if any. But that might be tough, especially since my new brother-in-law was her stepbrother.

Instead of going inside the church to change into my street clothes and leave as I had planned, my legs seemed to have a mind of their own. They propelled me across the

11

parking lot to the little party of five where Lori stood with her back to me, still stiff and unyielding.

My mother saw me, put her arm through mine, and pulled me into their group.

Seeing who had joined them, Lori rolled her eyes, looked skyward and exhaled an exaggerated breath while crossing her arms.

Smiling, I wondered if she was going to explode.

"Is there something wrong, dear?" Audrey, her mother, stared at her oddly, effectively directing everyone's attention on Lori.

Her face turned pink like earlier. I could tell she was working hard to hide her loathing, while she avoided looking at me.

Bravo!

"Nothing's wrong. Just a little tired. In fact, I believe I'll go change and gather my things and head home."

Seems the little darlin' isn't as immune to me as she'd like to make me believe. Being able to rile her temper was more fun than I'd had in years.

Oh, yeah. I was going to have more fun tormenting her the next time we met.

"I was telling Audrey and Jim they should come to Sunday dinner." My mother looked over sweetly to Lori. "And you should come too, dear. Nothing fancy, just home cooking."

"I-I—"

"We'd all love to come." Audrey gave her daughter a pointed look. "What can I bring?" She smiled back sweetly at my mother.

"Oh, don't worry about bringing anything. I've got it covered. We'll eat around one."

Mom loosened her hold on my arm effectively giving me a chance to escape.

12

"I'll see you tomorrow then." Lori smiled pleasantly at everyone without looking in my direction before storming off.

"I'll walk with you." I jogged to catch up with her.

"Oh, great. Just what I needed. Another round with Pretty Boy Floyd. Shoot me now and put me out of my misery." The words were said under her breath as she practically galloped to get away.

Chuckling, I easily fell in step with her.

When we were sufficiently far enough from our parents not to be heard, I said, "It looks like we will be seeing a lot more of one another, being family and all."

"Don't bet on it. And family? We're not even distant cousins."

"Maybe we're what they call *kissing cousins.*" My grin stretched across my face.

"Not in this life or the next to come."

"You wound me." I clutched my chest, chuckling.

"Look, I don't know why you feel it's your mission in life to torment me, but you can just back off." She reached to open the church door.

I beat her to it, which I could tell irked her. "After you, Princess." I gave a quasi-bow, smiling.

"How can Whitney be so loveable and you so loathsome?"

"Stick around, Sweetheart, I'll grow on you."

"Never." She gave me a pointed look. "Listen, because of Adam and Whitney, whom I love dearly, I will do my best to be civil to you. But beyond that, don't expect more. Do I make myself clear, or do I need to spell it out for you?"

"Ah, aren't you going to treat me even a little bit friendly?"

"Not if I can help it," Lori grounded out through clenched teeth.

13

"Ah, come on now. You'll find I'm not all that bad once you get to know me."

We were approaching the room where Lori and the other bridesmaids had changed clothes for the wedding.

"Mr. Singleton, I—"

"Seth."

She gave me a strange look, causing a break in her stride. "What?"

"Mr. Singleton is my dad. I'm Seth. Like you, Princess, I wish to be called Seth."

"You want to be called Seth, yet I'm called princess, sweetheart, darlin' or whatever name comes to your mind. *Humph*. Two can play this game."

By her acidly sweet smile, I knew she was up to something, and it wouldn't be pretty. I kept a straight face while laughing on the inside.

Pushing the door open, she walked in. "Have a pleasant life, if you can, *Studley*."

The door slammed in my face.

Unable to contain myself, I burst out laughing. Before I moved away from the door, I leaned in and said loud enough to ensure she heard me. "See you later, Sugar Pie."

I walked away whistling "Here Comes The Bride." I couldn't be for certain, but I thought I heard something hit the door, which caused my laughter to ring out in the hall all the more.

If I weren't a Police Detective and hadn't already vowed to stay single until I took a desk job, if ever, it might be fun to see just how far Lori would go to keep me at arm's length. The little gal certainly knew how to give back in spades.

A vision of snapping blue eyes, filled with fire, had me smiling.

Maybe, just maybe … I shook my head. Those thoughts would do nothing but lead me into deep trouble without the ability to extricate myself. I had no time to deal with women, especially this fiery-tempered spit-of-a-girl.

Still, it got under my skin that she didn't like me. There were few women who weren't attracted to me, or, at least, interested.

Lori was different. She didn't seem the slightest bit affected by me, making her a challenge. But if I went down that road, I'd have to watch my step. I couldn't go so far as to get her seeing me as a possible love interest.

Yup, I'd have to walk a fine line if I did what I was thinking.

Nothing was stopping me, outside of Whitney tearing into me if she ever found out. What harm could there be in having a little fun? Lori seemed able to hold her own, so it wouldn't be like I'd be picking her on, would it?

Who knows, once she got passed her anger, Lori and I might become good friends. Something one could never have in abundance. After all, we were nearly related. We shouldn't be at odds.

Who was I fooling? Princess would have me in deep trouble before I knew it if I did what I was thinking of doing.

No, it would be better to stay as far away as possible from lovely little Lori Morgan.

Chapter 2

Lori

Like a bothersome Texas chigger, Seth Singleton was causing me indescribable amounts of irritation. Why I allow him to do so, I didn't have a clue. Except to say, good manners dictated politeness, regardless if the man was galling. When I got around him, he could always get my blood boiling. He had a knack for getting under my skin.

I knew better than to let his words affect me. Nonetheless, around him, it was hard to keep a level head. He always drew the worst out of me, extracting his several pounds of flesh while brightly smiling.

Five days a week, all day long, I could handle a classroom full of high-spirited children. Why couldn't I handle one infuriating man?

I felt utterly drained after our encounters. I didn't like being snippy with anyone, especially when that someone was a quasi-relative. Come to think of it, he wasn't a relative. Not even a *close* kissing cousin of the worse kind.

"I'm leaving now." Joann was the last bridesmaid to leave besides me.

Seeing her hands full, I moved to open the door. "Here let me get that for you."

"Oh, thanks. I hope we can get together again real soon."

"Yeah. That would be nice." Seeing her shift the load in her arms, I asked, "Do you need some help out to your car?"

"No, I can get it. But hey, I'm sorry about Whitney's brother, Seth. I know he bothered the snot out of you. But he is awfully cute, and he does seem to have a thing for you." She winked.

"Well, I *don't* have a thing for him. In fact, I'd be happy if I never saw him again. How Whitney could turn out so nice, and him so ill-mannered, I'll never know."

"If you don't want him, send him my way."

I snorted. "You'd disown me as a friend if I did."

"I doubt it. He's one hunk of a guy." Joann smiled. "Later."

I closed the door knowing what Joann had said was true. Seth was a good-looking man, but he'd have to work long and hard on his attitude before I'd look at him twice. I was still puzzled why he seemed to have put me in his sights as someone to torment.

Like the little boys at school who loved to torment the girls and wouldn't leave them alone, that was Seth. And to think I would have to sit through dinner with him on Sunday.

I let loose a growl, wishing I could come up with some plausible reason to stay home.

Yanking down the zipper on my dress, I stripped the sleeves from my arms before realizing I shouldn't be taking my temper out on the garment. Seth was the culprit who deserved my wrath. Not this harmless, lovely dress Whitney had picked out for her bridesmaids, which surprisingly I liked.

I shimmied out of the gown, allowing it to slip to the floor. For the first time, I was able to breathe, really breathe. I slipped into my jeans, pulled the sweater over my head, and then took the hairpins from my hair. Shaking the

17

strands loose to tumble down my back, made me feel free and exhilarated, as if I were allowing all thoughts of Seth to fly from my mind.

My thoughts turned to my brother and his new wife. I'd been correct. Whitney and Adam were made for each other. And now they were married and on their way to ... only Adam and the ticket agent knew for sure. Adam wanted to keep their destination a secret so Whitney wouldn't have any hint where they were going.

One day, I hoped I would find someone as equally matched for me. But if not, I shrugged, remembering the near disasters of my past. I'd be okay with what I had.

Fortunately, I loved my teaching job. And I had family in abundance and many friends—well, one could never have enough friends, but the ones I did have, I wouldn't trade.

And then there was Robbie, with his expectant black eyes eager to please and give me plenty of love. My Scottish terrier was an excellent companion. He never sassed or made me feel inferior unlike ... *let it go. I am truly blessed, so what more could I ask for?*

Sliding the dress onto the hanger and into the garment bag, I grabbed it, my tote, and purse before leaving. Arms full, I opened the door, stopped to take one final look back at the room to ensure I had left nothing behind, and then stepped out into the hall.

Out of nowhere, a linebacker hit me. Somehow our feet got tangled, our heads banged together as we landed on the floor, in a heap. The guy ended up spread-eagle, landing on the top of me.

My breath whooshed out of my lungs. I pushed against his rock solid chest trying to get him off of me. When he didn't budge, I thought he might have been knocked out, that is, until he started chuckling.

The laugh was too familiar as the mellow woodsy smell filled the air around me.

Oh, great! This wasn't a linebacker. Sprawled all over me was none other than Seth Singleton, my nemesis.

This time, I punched the heels of my palms into his chest, which didn't affect him in the least.

"Would you please get off of me?"

"What a spoil-sport you are. I was kind of enjoying it, Princess."

He wiped the smile off his face and scrambled backward when he saw my flare of anger and the pain in my eyes.

"I'm sorry. Are you hurt?"

The concern in his voice had me shoving the few strands of hair out of my face. I came nose-to-nose with Seth. I peered into dark brown eyes framed by thick, black lashes any woman would die for, even me. And those rugged good looks, with his scruffy beard, goodness. Were his lips as soft and kissable as they looked?

What am I thinking? The hit on my head had to be the only answer for my lack of rational thought.

"Lori, are you hurt?" He touched my arm.

I shrugged him off. "Yes, I'm hurt. You would be too if you were my size and just had a two hundred pound ox land on top of you."

"One eighty-five." He hiked one brow, wearing that sarcastic smirk he was so fond of showing.

"Semantics." I brushed his retort aside like a pesky fly, doing my best to sit up.

He gripped both of my arms, this time, pulling me in an upright sitting position on the cold, hard tile floor. His touch sent a tingling sensation through my body when it shouldn't have registered at all. I didn't want to feel anything for this man who delighted in torturing me.

"I'm fine. Let go of me." I jerked free, and cold settled where the warmth of his hands had been.

I'm going crazy, plain and simple.

"What did you think you were doing charging down the hall like a linebacker?"

"Linebacker? You're the one who ran into me." He shook his head. "You came careening out the door like you were going to a last minute sale at Macy's."

"You're an imbecile."

"Takes one to know one, Sweetheart."

His cocky response infuriated me even more, if that were possible. I tried to scoot back to gain distance from him, but cried out in agony. Pain shot up my ankle through my leg and caused my stomach to revolt. I swallowed the gunk that came up in my throat, feeling worse for doing so.

"You're hurt. Where?" Alarm registered in his eyes. He glanced down at my legs.

After a deep breath to calm my stomach, I hissed out, "What, nothing hateful to say, just all gentle concern now?"

"I am concerned." He pinned me with his gaze, his brow furrowed. "You can't believe I did this on purpose."

"Ha! I—" I was caught up short when his hands gently probed my lower leg and ankle. When he found the injured spot, I couldn't keep from taking an indrawn hiss. "Uh! Don't. Please."

"I'm going to have to take your boot off to examine your foot." He waited for my consent.

I nodded.

"But first, let me scoot you back against the wall so you'll have something to lean against."

"I can ... ouch!" Tears filled my eyes.

"No, you can't. Now will you allow me to help?"

Seeing his sincere concern, I nodded. I hated feeling helpless and obligated to this man.

20

He stood, bending over me and placed his hands under my arm. Lifting me slightly, he slid me back against the wall.

I just hoped my deodorant was still holding. I would hate for him to wrinkle his nose or say *P.U.* if it weren't. Knowing him, that's exactly what he'd do.

His touch on my calf, though nothing sensual, gave me cause for concern. I was beginning to feel things I shouldn't feel for Seth even through the pain.

Without looking up at me, he unzipped the side of my boot. "This is going to hurt. Your ankle is already swelling."

"Then this will be right down your alley. You love to torture me. Just do it."

A flash of regret was the only sign my words had hit pay dirt. Had I truly been that awful?

Ignoring my outburst, he took hold of my leg and the heel of the boot. With particular care, he pulled the shoe off, amazingly gentle, causing little pain.

I was being a jerk, and I knew it, but I allowed my anger to fight back the softening of my heart. *Seth.* Of all people, I didn't want to feel anything, especially desire where he was concerned.

"Your ankle may be broken. I need to get you to a doctor."

"I'll be fine. Just help me to my car."

"Not on my watch, Princess."

"*LORI,*" I ground out, even though I liked hearing all the pet names he called me.

His chuckle, instead of angering me, dissolved some of the animosity I had hidden deep inside.

"While we're at it, I believe I need my head x-rayed too."

Brushing aside my bangs, his fingers gently probed the tender spot where our foreheads had collided. His look of concern was almost my undoing.

"You have a small bump, but I don't think it's anything serious. But after the doctor is through checking your ankle, we'll get him to look at your head."

"No, I'm sorry. My head is fine. You're right. It's only a bump." Something in his look had me reevaluating my snarkiness. "Can we start over?"

His puzzled gaze had me smiling and holding out my hand.

"Hi, I'm Lori Morgan. I believe we have something in common. My brother, Adam, and your sister, Whitney, got married today."

A grin of pure delight stretched across his face, healing the wounds his words had caused in my heart.

Engulfing my hand in his, he shook it once but held on.

Looking into his sparkling dark eyes, I knew I was in deep trouble. I would have been better off staying snarky.

"Glad to make your acquaintance Lori. I'm Seth Singleton." He chuckled. "Now do you think it will be all right if I pick you up and carry you to my Jeep. We need to get your ankle looked at by a doctor."

"Since it seems I can't walk, then I guess you'll have to carry me." I looked at the things scattered around the hall. "What about our stuff?"

"I'll get you settled in my Jeep, then come back for our things."

"That works for me." Already my ankle had doubled in size, causing more pain than I could imagine.

He pulled his keys from his leather jacket and bent toward me. One arm slipped beneath my knees, and the other around my back. And then as if I didn't weigh more than a newborn babe, he lifted me, holding me close to his chest, our faces inches away.

22

The thought occurred to me to raise my hand and touch his scruffy beard to see how it felt against my palm—rough? Scratchy?

"And what happened here?"

I jerked like I'd been shot from a cannon. My face turned hot, no doubt crimson red, as if caught in a crime.

Seth's hold on me tightened, as his soft chuckle fanned my already hot cheeks.

Pastor Lakeland, with questionable look on his face, was watching us as he approached.

"Good evening, Pastor Steve. Lori has either sprained or broken her ankle, I don't know which. I'm taking her to a Doc-in-the-box." He looked at me. "Either that or the emergency, whichever she prefers."

Pastor Steve came closer and then whistled through his teeth. "That looks painful. How did it happen?"

"My fault entirely."

I was shocked to hear Seth take the blame. "No, it was my—"

"Lori was coming out of the dressing room. I didn't see her until it was too late. We collided. Her injury probably happened when our legs got twisted together." He winked at me. "Or when I fell on top of her. Can't be sure."

"I was as much to blame."

"Afraid not." Seth shook his head as he tightened his hold. "But we should leave and get you to that doctor."

"Do you need help carrying her?" Pastor Steve looked at the stuff on the floor.

"No. I've got it covered."

Covered? I'll say. My blood rushed through my veins. My heart pumped like I was in the throws of a heart attack.

I was too young to be having a heart attack. My reactions had to be because of Seth. My senses were reeling and going off the chart and in front of our pastor, no less.

23

"You go on. Take her to the car. I'll pick up your things and bring them out to you." Pastor Steve began gathering our stuff.

"Thanks, that will save time." Seth began moving toward the exit. "I'll drive her in my Jeep. One of my buddies and I will swing by later to get Lori's Mini Cooper."

"You won't have to do that. I can drive it myself after they've looked at my foot."

How did Seth know I had a Mini Cooper? What else did he know about me?

"Believe me, the way your ankle is swelling, you won't be driving for a while, especially since it's your right leg."

"He's correct, you know." Pastor Steve said from behind us.

I didn't want to know, but in my heart I knew what Seth had said would probably be the case.

He carried me down the long hall out into the crisp winter air. Darkness had descended. Thankfully, there were only a few cars left in the parking lot, but no people standing around. I didn't want others to witness my embarrassment.

"I can't be stranded." I sounded like a whiney child even to my ears.

When I shivered, he pulled me up tighter, hunching over me, doing his best to shield me from the cold wind.

"You won't be. Either one of my buddies or I can drive you anywhere you need to go."

"No. That won't be necessary. Mom will be able to drive me around for a few days until my ankle's better."

The chirp of his alarm alerted me we had reached his car. He opened the door, then shifted me in his arms. "Can you stand on your good foot and lean against the side of my Jeep while I get a blanket from the back?"

"Sure. I'll be okay. But I don't need a blanket."

Without saying a word, he lowered me against his shiny black Jeep, making sure I could stand on my own.

"I'll be right back."

"I really don't ..." He'd already left me and was rummaging in the backend.

He came back with a soft, fleecy blanket and began spreading it out on the seat throwing half of it over the back.

The blanket got me wondering why he carried one in his car in the first place. I figured with his looks he was no doubt a chick magnet. But really, a soft fleecy blanket? I felt sure I wasn't the first nor would I be the last to stretch out on that blanket.

A tinge of the old green monster raised its ugly head. I kicked myself mentally.

This is Seth. Not a man you want to become interested in or date.

"I think you'll be far more comfortable riding in the back with your leg stretched out."

"I'm not sure I can climb—"

My words were cut off as he swished me up into his strong arms again. He leaned us into the back seat area and placed me gently on the bench. When his face barely grazed my cheek, causing his scruffy beard to tickle my skin, he hesitated. His dark eyes connected with mine and then turned agitated as if I was inconvenience.

Reaching across me, he pulled the blanket over my legs and up around my arms.

"There that should help to keep you warm." He raised a brow. "And for your information, which I shouldn't have to explain, the blanket is a gift I got for Christmas. Not for the reasons you were thinking."

"I wasn't thinking—"

The door slammed, successfully cutting off any untruth I was about to perpetrate.

25

He walked around and got into the driver's seat, his face a mask.

The front passenger door opened distracting me.

Pastor Steve put our things on the seat and floor.

"I pray it's nothing serious. Hopefully, it can be healed with a little rest and getting off your feet for a few days."

Still stinging from Seth's rebuke, I smiled at Pastor Steve. "Thanks for your help. I'm sure it will."

"Don't bet on it," my companion snorted. "Thanks, Steve, I'll be sure to let you know what the prognosis is once we find out. See you in the morning."

"Please do. I'll be praying for you, Lori. Have a safe journey."

Though I was in the back and Seth in the front, his Jeep felt terribly small and confining. I was in a car with a man, minutes ago, I disliked with a passion. It appeared I wasn't so indifferent to him after all.

"Where to, Princess, a doc-in-the-box or the hospital emergency?"

I huffed out, "A 24-hour emergency clinic will do."

"Sure thing."

Silence prevailed except for the sound of the engine and road noise. Seth maneuvered his Jeep through the traffic with finesse, while I did my best to keep my injured ankle perfectly still.

It was a shame we were like sandpaper, ready to rub each other raw at a moment's notice. When he showed his softer side, something I didn't know existed until we collided in the hall, he could make me feel special, like the princess he enjoyed calling me. But I knew it would only be a matter of time before he riled my temper again.

True, Seth would make some woman a good husband, just not me.

Chapter 3

Seth

The drive, though short, was strained and silent. With Lori's tendency for a short fuse where I was concerned, I wasn't sure if she was upset with me again or not. One thing for sure, I wasn't about to find out. I figured I wouldn't push it, not wanting a verbal rematch of earlier, even if I did get pleasure out of our sparring matches.

I couldn't remember when I'd had such fun teasing someone of the opposite sex. However, in her injured state, I wasn't about to get her all riled up. Plenty of time for that later.

I smiled, wondering if she enjoyed our little rows as much as I did. *Probably not.*

As the lights from the street streaked by, from my rearview mirror I saw the pained look on her face. Though I did my best to miss the bumps and potholes, some of the jolting couldn't be helped, especially in my Jeep rigged for off-road fun.

"Hang in there. The 24-hour emergency care is on the next block."

"I'm good." Lori grimaced again. She closed her eyes, leaning her head against the exterior wall of the Jeep.

Hearing her moan, I knew she was anything but fine.

I whipped into the parking lot, stopping under the portico, and then turned back to look at her. "I'll go inside and get a wheelchair. Wait in the car."

By the time I rounded the front of the Jeep, Lori had her door already open. Her bottom lip was firmly held between her teeth as she attempted to slip out of the car and down onto the pavement.

Before her foot could hit the ground, I scooped her up in my arms. Like earlier, I wasn't prepared for the reaction I received with Lori being up against my chest.

"I can walk." She stiffened her body and clamped her jaw tight against another spasm of pain.

"Not likely." I made sure my grip on her was solid, hating how my emotions were getting all mixed up where she was concerned.

"Why is it men need to show a woman how macho they can be?"

Oh, yeah. This woman delights in baiting me.

"For your information, I'm not showing off. Common sense dictates I carry you to keep you from injuring your ankle further." I mumbled the rest, "You're too stubborn to wait in the car while I go inside for a wheelchair."

Her *humph* resonated into my chest.

"You don't have to be ugly about it." She crossed her arms and stiffened more, sending a signal she wanted distance.

I laughed. "Lady, you have a stubborn streak in you a block wide and a mile long." I shifted her in my arms to carry her better. *Bad move.* "Why don't you just relax and enjoy the ride."

"I'm not stubborn."

"You could have fooled me." My huff dislodged some of the irritation Lori always seemed capable of arousing.

The automatic doors swished open, and the warm air rushed out, mingling with the cold night breeze.

Lori shivered. "You can let me down now. I'm perfectly capable of hobbling to the desk."

"Nope. No can do." I quirked my brow, smiling. "You can sit in this chair. I'll let them know why you're here. No need putting more stress on your ankle than need be."

"Really. This is ridiculous. I—"

Without further ado, I deposited her in a two-seater bench so she could prop her leg up. "Like I say to my little niece Mandy, *Shush, the doctor is going to make your boo-boo much better*. Now sit there and be quiet."

She looked ready to tear into me. Instead, she gave an unladylike snort of disdain.

All the people in the waiting room were watching us.

One man smiled at me and gave a *thumbs-up*.

I nodded.

"Honey, don't fight it. Your husband knows best." The little gray-haired lady sitting next to Lori was knitting something long and bizarre looking.

"Oh, no! He's not—"

"Men just love to fuss over us when we're not feeling well. My dear Herbert was that way when he was on this earth. So enjoy it while you can." She gave Lori a conspirator's wink.

"You should listen to the lady, Princess. She seems to know what she's talking about." After winking at Lori and the woman, I said, "Make sure she stays put for me, will you?"

"You go on. I'll look after your wife."

Chuckling, I sauntered off toward the check-in desk.

"Honey, it appears you have one good man there."

"He's one good man I could do without," Lori muttered.

"I heard that."

Several disguised chuckles from around the room could be heard.

29

The young girl behind the counter definitely wasn't giving me the cold shoulder like Lori, just the opposite. She didn't look much older than eighteen. And though somewhat attractive, I plainly wasn't interested.

Once I told her what we were here for, she gave me papers to fill out and asked for an insurance card or a form of payment. Not knowing what the costs would be, I whipped out my credit card and told her to put the charges on it, hoping it wouldn't be too high. But I was determined to pay for her care since I was the one who collided into her.

"Here, *Sweetheart*." Smiling, I held out the clipboard waiting on Lori to react. "You will need to fill out these papers."

Without a word, she snatched the board out of my hands, the only show of irritation my little endearment had gotten to her.

I glanced around the room, sizing up the occupants. Not sure what I expected to see—criminals, deviants. Everyone looked normal, if sick people can be called normal. I wondered what we'd pick up from this coughing, sneezing bunch, or the ones holding their stomach. Hopefully, nothing.

"We've got about a twenty minute plus wait before the doc will see you."

A grunt was the only acknowledgment I received. Seeing an empty chair a couple down from Lori, I moved toward the seat.

"Oh, no." The little lady by Lori began gathering her things. "You sit down here by your lady."

"I'm not his lady."

I shook my head, waving for her to remain seated. "I think I'm better off down here." I winked. "Since I caused her injury, she's none too happy with me."

The door to the inner chambers opened and out walked a woman with a little boy about six, his arm in a sling.

"You can have my chair." The man on the other side of Lori stood. "It looks like we're ready to leave."

"Thank you, sir." I nodded toward his child. "I hope he's a fast healer."

He chuckled. "I do too. Otherwise, I'll be doing double duty, since it was my fault."

My ears perked up. "Oh, what happened?" I tried to look sympathetic as I searched for any tell-tail signs of dishonesty in the man.

"Oh, you know how women are." He looked over at Lori.

"Yeah, I sure do." I nodded in agreement.

"She's always telling me I'm too rough with the boy. But you can't let a boy become a pantywaist either. At least, not in today's world. They'll eat him alive. You know what I mean? I keep telling him, he's gotta stick up for himself."

"Sure do. It's tough out there." Again I smiled, mentally taking note of the dad as a suspect for child abuse.

"Exactly. The kid bruises too easily."

"I hear yah." I stuck out my hand. "Oh, by the way, I'm Seth Singleton."

He took my hand and gave a firm handshake. "Oscar Wilder."

"Nice to meet you, Oscar. You live around here close?"

"Yeah." He narrowed his eyes.

I turned to Lori. "We live about five miles from here. Like you, we were roughhousing around when she sprained her ankle. Or at least, I hope it's not broken. I'll have the devil to pay if it is. You know what I mean?"

"Oh, yeah. We live a few blocks off Greenville Avenue. Been there going on ten years. I told my Missus, it was high time we moved. The neighbors are getting too noisy and want to butt into our business. Can't have that."

"Ain't that the truth?"

"We're ready."

A mousy-haired woman walked up. She avoided looking at me. The little boy stood back behind her, and though curious, he didn't say a word. He just watched his father.

"What have I told you about interrupting me?" Oscar's eyes narrowed, his mouth tightened and pulled to the left as his chin rose slightly.

"Sorry." The woman moved back. She lowered her chin to her chest as she put her arm around the little boy, then bent to say something in her son's ear.

"It was nice meeting you. But as you can see, the little woman's anxious to get home."

After nodding at Mrs. Wilder, I looked at the boy. "I hope you get to feeling better real soon."

His mother nudged him without looking at her husband or me. "Peter, what do you say?"

"Thank you, sir."

"You're welcome." I looked at Oscar. "Be careful driving home."

"Will do. Nice talking with you." He put his hand sideways to his mouth and leaned in close to my ear. "You've got a real live wire on your hands with that one." He laughed, nodding in Lori's direction before motioning to his wife to head on out.

I followed them to the door. When she was about to push it open, I said, "Here let me get that for you."

When I stepped outside with them, Wilder looked at me oddly.

Smiling, I said, "It's a little stuffy in there, if you get my meaning. A few seconds out here should do the trick."

"I hear yah." His laugh sounded rusty from little use.

32

The family walked off toward a late model black Ford. Wilder got into the driver's seat and turned on the engine. Mrs. Wilder helped the boy in the back seat and got him buckled up, while Wilder, using some rather choice words, yelled at her to hurry up and shut the door.

Memorizing the license place, I gave them a two-finger salute goodnight. I waited until they drove off before walking back in the building.

Once inside, I sat in Wilder's vacated chair, pulled out a little notebook and pen from the inside pocket of my jacket. I wrote down the license number, name, and what I observed before putting them back in my pocket.

Feeling a tug on my arm, I turned to face Lori.

"You think he's abusive, don't you?" She had leaned toward me, whispering.

"Not sure." I shrugged. "But it won't hurt to have it checked out."

She cocked her head to one side while staring at me.

"What? You don't like my looks?" I smiled.

"No, it's not that. You're never off the job are you?"

"Never. I'm on 24/7, regardless where I am, or whom I'm with. That's why I'm still single." I raised my brow, smiling. "And I like it that way."

She gave that unladylike snort again. "I can think of a million more reasons why you're single. And your job wouldn't be one of them."

"Whatever." I pointed at the clipboard with all her personal information. "Are you through with that?"

She handed it to me. "Yes, thank you."

I stood, moved to the counter, giving the young girl a huge, charming smile, handing her the clipboard.

"It'll be a few more minutes." She looked from her computer screen to me, giving me a seductive smile.

On second thought, I might have been wrong about her. She had to be older than she looked.

"I'm in no hurry." Again, I gave her my winning smile. "Have you worked here long?"

She sat up straight in her chair, pushing her shoulders back, showing off her assets. "Only a couple of weeks."

"That's nice. You plan on getting into the field of medicine? Or are you a person who likes the challenge of the front office?"

"I like the front office. I get to meet a lot of interesting people on this job … like you." She winked at me.

Lady, you're barking up the wrong alley.

"By the way, my name is Seth." I pointed back at Lori. "She's a relative of mine."

"Oh, that's nice." She flirted some more. "I'm Brandy."

"Hmm, your name will be easy to remember. I already had you down as a *smooth* voice, *brandy* colored hair, and a *warm and inviting* personality."

"Why that's sweet. What do you do? I bet it's something interesting." She batted her eyelashes.

"That's where you're wrong. My job is quite predictable and filled with more paperwork than I like. But hey"—I shrugged for effect—"we can't always have everything we want, if you get my meaning."

"I know what you mean. But sometimes you can have just *exactly* what you want."

Man, was this one ever on the prowl.

"*Hmm.*" I let her think what she would. "Oh, by the way, my buddy Oscar was going to give me his address and phone number, but we got to talking, and he forgot. We haven't seen each other, like forever." I wrinkled my nose.

She gave me a puzzled look.

"Oscar Wilder. You know, the one that just left with his wife and son, Peter."

"Oh, yeah, that guy." The young girl scrutinized me, like she couldn't picture the two of us as bosom buds.

34

"*Man*, he sure has changed. Would you believe it, we are much the same age."

"Couldn't be."

Her shocked expression was priceless.

"Yeah, it's a shame how he's let himself go. Now me …" I shrugged. "Well, anyway, we were supposed to meet up Monday night, but after he left, I remembered I have an appointment already. You wouldn't be able to give me his number would you?" I raised my brows, knowing she was on the verge of saying no. "Ah, come on, please. You can do this one little favor for me, can't you?"

"I really can't. I could lose my job."

"Well, I wouldn't want to do anything to jeopardize your employment here. I can see how much you like it."

Looking over at the door, she cleared her throat, while her fingertips turned an invoice toward me, and then her black-painted nail tapped the sheet several times.

I took one of the clinic's cards, turned it over and hurriedly wrote the address, and telephone number down. "Hey, it's been a pleasure getting to know you."

"Here's my phone number and address." She scribbled her information rather hurriedly and then handed me the slip of paper. "Maybe we can get together sometime for coffee or drinks, or whatever." She shrugged, smiling suggestively.

"You never know. But I've got your number. Thanks again, Brandy."

When I returned to my chair, Lori gave me the eagle eye.

"Did you get what you were after?"

"Yes." I flashed Brandy's telephone number at her. "And then some. The young lady gave me her number."

"Why am I not surprised? I bet you get that quite often in your line of work."

"Not bragging, but unlike you, most women are attracted to me."

"*Humph*. Must be the badge. It certainly can't be your *winning* personality."

"Honey, you just don't know the half."

A nurse in turquoise scrubs stood at the door with a wheelchair. "Lori Morgan."

"Your chariot has arrived. I think that's our cue."

Chapter 4

Lori

To say I was a pretty picture would be a misnomer. A book, the remote, and magazines were in easy reach from my position on the couch. I lounged in my pj's, earbuds in my ears, talking to my mom.

The mound of pillows elevating my leg was precarious at best. The Ace bandage along with an ice pack surrounded my injured ankle and chilled me to the bone.

Lovely! Not.

"Thankfully, it was only a sprain." I adjusted the pillow behind my neck.

"I think you should stay with us for a while. At least, until your ankle is better."

My mother's concern was touching, but I wasn't budging from my apartment.

"No. I'll be fine. But I appreciate you taking care of Robbie for me. I hope he isn't going to be an inconvenience."

"He isn't. In fact, Jim has already taken him out for a walk twice today."

"Good. It should only be for a week, two at the most. I'm just glad I have this next week off. Hopefully, I'll get the hang of walking with crutches and be ready to go back to school when Christmas break is over. I'm maneuvering better, especially after Seth put extra padding on the armrests."

"Seth ... *hmm*. Now, *there's* a man. And handsome, too. You couldn't go wrong—"

"Mom, don't go there." Though she couldn't see me, I rolled my eyes.

"All I'm saying ..."

"Yes, I know. I hear you loud and clear." I breathed in, then exhaled loudly.

I didn't want to have this conversation, but have it I must.

"Seth is nice, but he isn't my type. I believe it's his mission in life to tick me off every time he opens his mouth. He can be so egotistical and irritating. And then when I least expect it, he turns sweet, like he did last night when I got injured."

I closed my eyes wishing I could erase the memory of his kindness, or how my senses went off the chart when he carried me in his arms. Even the remembrance of his manly scent had me careening down a path I was clawing and fighting not to take.

"No doubt, he'll make some woman a lovely husband. That woman's just not me."

"'The lady doth protest too much, me thinks.'" Mom's quote of Shakespeare came across loud and strong.

"No, I'm stating the facts precisely, so you won't go all bonkers on me and become a matchmaker mama on a mission."

Mom gave me a stern look, and then smiled. "If you think about it, dear. You couldn't go wrong with a man like Seth."

I unclenched my teeth. "I know you mean well. But Seth and I are two individuals who are diametrically opposed." I huffed, letting some of the steam out.

"Call me old fashioned. But I'd rather fall in love with the man I marry, not want to kill him every time he opens his mouth."

Mom's tinkling laughter had me smiling in spite of the fact thoughts of Seth could incur my wrath and longing at the same time. *I must have injured more than my foot.*

"I need to let you go. It's time for another pain pill."

"You're not taking too many of those pills, are you? You know what happened to—"

"Mom, it's Advil. Nothing more."

"Oh, all right then. You rest, dear. We'll be by after church to check on you and bring you some lunch and then head on over to the Singletons for lunch with them."

"You don't need to, but it'll be nice to see you. Thanks. I love you."

"I love you too, dear. But you might want to reconsider. Seth's quite a catch."

"Mom—" I was talking to the room. The woman had hung up on me.

A knock on the door pulled my attention away from Mom's persistence of Seth. I carefully scooted my foot off the pillows, swung it around to the floor. A twinge of pain had me sucking in air. I slipped my robe on before grabbing the crutches.

Another insistent knock had me yelling, "Just a minute. I'm coming."

I stood in front of the door, trying my best to look through the peephole but to no avail. "Who is it?"

"It's me. Let me in. I brought you breakfast."

"Seth?" I unlocked the door and hobbled back awkwardly.

"Were you expecting someone else?" He walked in carrying a stack of white boxes.

His dazzling smile left me speechless. The mix of woodsy cologne and food smells did a number on me. And those dark eyes surrounded with thick black lashes ... *goodness*.

It was too early for Seth.

Whoa, down girl! This is Seth—you know, the one who dearly loves to annoy you at every turn. Not some hunk out of a novel.

"Just surprised to see you. I figured-ah-well, that you'd be on your way to church or something." I moved back, allowing him to enter.

"I am. But I have plenty of time. And since I was a contributing factor for your injury, I figured the least I could do is to make sure you're fed."

He flashed me another adorable smile and then breezed into the apartment. His kinetic energy had me reeling.

"Listen, you don't owe me anything, and you don't have to do penance." I pushed the door shut and hobbled after him. Already my ankle was throbbing.

"No penance here. I brought comfort food—sausage rolls, kolaches, and donuts."

"Smells wonderful. Thank you."

He turned and gave me a stern look. "Just where do you think you're going? Go sit down and get your foot propped up. I'll bring the food to you." He waited for me to comply before moving into the kitchen. "You want milk, juice, tea, or coffee?"

"Milk with my donut. Tea with my kolaches."

"Boy, aren't we picky."

I started to tell him he could take his smart-alecky self out of my apartment, but his teasing look stopped me.

"I don't know if *we* are picky, but, yes, I am. And I'm opinionated too."

He chuckled. "I think I already knew that."

Settled back on the sofa with my foot propped up, I watched Seth in my kitchen poking into cabinets and drawers. He had no hesitation or awkwardness, and he moved with the ease and confidence of a man who knew what he was about.

When he wasn't tormenting me, he could be quite charming. And like Mom had mentioned, Seth was handsome, even with his scruffy beard. Today, in particular, his blue shirt and pullover sweater beneath his leather jacket set off his dark good looks.

And those jeans? They should be outlawed. No man had a right to look as good as Seth.

Where did that come from? This is Seth, remember? If I had been taking any, I would have blamed my lapse on the strong pain meds.

"Do you have a tray?"

He caught me staring and looked a little confused.

"What?" My cheeks warmed.

A deep crease between his brows appeared. "A breakfast tray ... to set your tea and food on?"

"*Mmm*, yes. In the pantry there." I pointed in the general vicinity, then turned to stare out the glass patio doors. I didn't want to be tempted to watch him. When it turned out to be too enticing not to sneak a peek, I closed my eyes.

"Are you in pain?"

I nearly jumped out of my skin. Seth was standing next to the sofa looking down at me, his face covered with concern.

"Not too bad. I was going to take some Advil before you came."

"I'll get it. Where is it?"

He scooted the coffee table next to the couch, moved the remote, book, and magazines over before looking around. "Ah, I see the bottle. One or two."

"Two. They don't take away all the pain, but it helps some."

"Where's your pain meds?"

41

"In the cupboard." I motioned. "But they make me feel odd. I don't like taking them unless my ankle's really hurting."

"I hear ya." He came back from the kitchen with the tray loaded with food and slid it on the coffee table. "Here, take these first, then we'll eat." Handing me a glass of water and the pills, he waited.

After popping the pills in my mouth, I asked, "Are you staying?"

He gave me an odd look. "Unless you'd rather I leave."

"No. I didn't mean that. Please stay." I motioned for him to sit down.

After pulling a chair over next to the coffee table, he handed me a paper plate and a napkin, then held out the box filled with donuts, and next the sausage rolls.

"Were you expecting company?"

A small wrinkle appeared between Seth's brows.

I motioned at the box with the two-dozen donuts. "There are enough donuts and rolls here to feed a small army."

His face cleared. "I wasn't sure what kind of donuts you'd like, so I bought several of my favorites—buttermilk and chocolate, and then had the girl throw in one of each of the others, just in case. There are fruit kolaches also."

"There's no way on earth I'll be able to eat more than one each."

His smile lit the room. "I'll take the leftovers to church and give them to Connie. The worship team will finish off what we don't eat."

"For a minute, you had me going. I figured you thought I was a big eater." I took a bite of my sausage roll, savoring the taste. When I swallowed, my curiosity got the best of me. "Who's Connie?"

"Connie Stevenson."

"Is she on the worship team?"

"Yeah. When you're mobile again, I'll introduce you. I think you'll like her. She's a close friend and colleague of mine."

I wanted to ask how close but knew it was none of my business. And why did I care anyway? It wasn't like I was interested in Seth.

"Connie's the one with long brown hair. She stands on the end to the left."

I remembered her. She was a cute brunette. Probably the sort of woman Seth gravitated towards. Nothing like me—blonde, and average in appearance, and passable in the looks department. And though only 5'4" I was taller than Connie. But then Seth was six foot plus, perfect height for me, if I were interested.

"What kind of work do you do?"

My attention jerked back to Seth. "Work?"

"Yeah, you know, the thing that pays your bills, puts food on the table." He glanced around the room. "Unless you're independently wealthy."

I laughed at his little quip and also to cover being caught off guard thinking about him.

"I'm a teacher. I work with children whose second language is English. I also have a couple of classes in English."

"Why that field?"

"My mother and grandmother were teachers, so it just felt natural to follow in their footsteps." I reached for a chocolate-chocolate donut. "And you? I know you're a police detective, but why that field?"

"There's always been something about trying to beat the bad guy at his own game that appealed to me. I guess it's the cops and robbers thing." He grinned.

He took a bite out of his donut, chewed, and then washed it down with coffee.

Watching him was irresistible. I could see the little boy in this grown man. Even envision him playing cops and robbers. But his job was no game. It was for real, and not always would he come out unscathed.

"I find the study of the criminal mind fascinating. To slap handcuffs on a drug dealer or pimp, or bring in a murderer when I know I have him dead to rights, gives me a rush. Most people don't understand and can only see the danger in my job. I see the whole picture with the end result ... getting the criminal off the street."

"I'll bet you're good at it too."

"I'd like to think so." He took another big gulp of his coffee, set it on the tray before standing.

"Listen, I meant what I said."

"About what?"

"I'm going to make sure you're taken care of this week. After church, I'll bring you lunch."

"There's no need. Mom and Jim are stopping by and bringing lunch. And as far as next week goes, that's not necessary either. Mom is tickled pink to be able to smother me with her mothering."

"Well, I'll still check up on you. Since this was my fault, the least I can do is to make sure you have a ride if you need to go some place."

"That's won't be necessary."

"It is to me." He held out his hand. "Are you through with that?"

"I'm not an invalid. I can clean up after myself. And listen, as far as the next couple of weeks, my mother will gladly take me where I need to go."

"Not on my watch." He gave me a look of determination before taking the plate out of my hand. "Would you like more tea before I go?"

"You're one infuriating man."

"Glad I can oblige." He displayed his cocky grin.

"Do you ever take no for an answer?"

"Not often." Again his gorgeous smile appeared.

I would have liked another cup of tea, but I wasn't about to ask for one. Instead, I figured I'd wait until Seth left, then I'd get it myself.

The shrilly whistle of the teakettle let me know Seth had already anticipated my desire for more tea.

I couldn't figure out what kind of man he was. One minute so irritating I felt like hitting him upside the head. The next, he was all kindness itself. I'd never get used to his mood swings.

Thankfully, he wasn't my concern. Without a doubt, his fondness for Connie would make her a far better choice.

Why did that thought leave a bitter taste in my mouth?

Chapter 5

Seth

I pulled into Grace Church parking lot and, because it was early, I found a parking spot up close. Instead of getting out and going in, I stared out the window at nothing in particular.

Lori had gotten past my defenses, but how? That wasn't like me. My rule … never get too close to any woman, period. Even though I dated from time to time, it was never serious and completely under control, at least on my part.

Thankfully, Lori's folks were bringing her lunch this afternoon. That relieved me from having to be around playing nursemaid for the remainder of the day.

Not that she wasn't good company, she was. But after last night and then this morning, I was beginning to experience more than friendship for her, and that bothered me. Like an irritating mosquito bite that itches something awful, that was Lori.

Attractive, with plenty of great qualities to recommend her. *If I were looking for a woman, which I'm not, Lori would be a good choice.* At this time in my life, I didn't need the distraction or temptation.

Best to keep my distance, which might prove to be a problem. We were bound to meet from time to time with her going to the same church and her stepbrother, Adam, married to my sister, Whitney.

Instead of checking in on her tomorrow, maybe I'd let her fend for herself as she asked. It sounded like her mother would be more than happy to play nursemaid. And she didn't act like she wanted me around.

Or maybe Tim wouldn't mind checking in on her. I'm sure he'd be more than happy to take her off my hands, and she might like him better than me.

That'll work.

A given. I would steer clear of Lori for a while. Get over this, whatever it was—I wouldn't call it an attraction exactly, more like a fascination—and get on with my life.

I snatched up the boxes of food and got out of my car. The cold north wind blasted me in the face, causing me to pick up speed. Thankfully, the chilly wind seemed to clear my head where Lori was concerned, making me more in control and on the right track again.

I walked into the church and down the hall to the practice room.

I'll call Tim right after church and explain the circumstances. Hopefully, he'll go with me to meet Lori and help her out until she could manage on her own. Yup! This was a good plan.

"Hey, Seth." Connie was heading in my direction. "Tell me there's food in those boxes."

"Sure is. I brought some donuts and sausage rolls for the gang." I grinned, knowing where I stood with Connie—friends only. Tim, my partner, had his eyes set on her.

"*Mmm*, my kind of guy. Hand 'em over." Connie, palms up, wiggled her fingers at me.

I snatched them back out of reach, teasing. "Can you be trusted?"

47

"Let's put it this way, if you don't hand over those boxes, I'll take you down and cuff you with your own handcuffs. So which will it be?" Her look said *I dare you to hold back.*

Laughing, I said, "You win."

She eyed the boxes hungrily before filching them out of my hands.

"Smart guy. I'll take care of these." She turned, heading for the table while I followed.

"Make sure you leave some for the others."

"I'm hungry, not a pig." She made a face and then waved the boxes in the air before setting them on the table. "Hey y'all, look what Seth brought."

After opening the lid, she took a deep sniff, before looking inside.

"Hey, you have no room to call me pig. Looks like you raided the boxes before you got here. Several are missing." She grabbed a napkin then pulled out a chocolate donut covered with sprinkles. Taking a huge bite, she closed her eyes and chewed.

It was a shame I wasn't intertested in Connie. As a Crime Scene Investigator, she knew the score and understood why I wasn't looking for attachments.

The statistics of my job were far better than years ago, but I still dealt with some unsavory characters. The gangs and drug dealers were of the worse kind. Their motto, *don't ask, kill first.*

I didn't want to subject the woman I married to worry or uncertainty. And the nine to sometimes twelve-hour days weren't exactly conducive for a happy home life either.

I felt a tug on my pant leg. Little three-year-old Jacob looked up at me, nearly falling over backward.

"Can I have one, pease?"

Scooping him up in my arms, I said, "You sure can, buddy. Let's go get one. Do you like sprinkles?"

Jake's nod caused his whole body to shake.

"I believe there's one with your name on it."

"Weally?" His eyes grew big.

"I believe so. Shall we have a look?"

"Wes, pease."

I leaned him over the box so he could see all his choices. He turned and looked at me.

"Go ahead. Get the one you want."

He reached in and grabbed the last chocolate covered sprinkles donut.

"Good choice, my man. Here's a napkin." I held one out to him.

His little fingers latched onto it while he took a big bite out of the donut. Icing and sprinkles coated his lips, some of the sprinkles escaped and rolled down onto my arm and then the floor.

Natalie, Jacob's mother, joined us. "What do you tell Detective Singleton?"

"Fank you."

"You're welcome."

He wiggled to get down. As soon as his feet hit the floor, he ran to his dad. He showed him his donut with a bite out of it, and then offered his dad a bite.

"Thanks, Seth." She nodded in her son's direction. "You'd make a great dad."

I didn't answer her, just shrugged.

"I don't suppose you've heard from Whitney and Adam?"

"Not a word. But I'm sure she'll be checking in with the folks sometime today."

"It certainly was a beautiful wedding." She raised her brow, and a teasing grin appeared. "When are you going to walk down the aisle?"

"Not you, too." I shook my head. "Cut me some slack. I get enough of that from my folks."

"All right. But I'm going to be on the lookout for a sweet girl, just for you."

"Don't do me any favors. I like my single status. And it's not likely to change anytime soon, not in the near or distant future."

"Never say never." She laughed as she glanced in her husband's direction. "I'd better go help Jake. Otherwise, little Jake will be a sticky mess. See you later."

"What was that all about?" Connie came up alongside me, linking her arm through mine.

"Same old, same old."

"Ah, let me guess. When are you going to get married and settle down?"

"Something like that." Seeing the sparkle in Connie's eyes, I knew I was in for it.

"Well, when are you?"

"Give it a rest. Or maybe I'll tell my partner, Tim, a certain secret?"

She punched me in the arm. "You better not."

I cocked my head to the side, scrutinizing her.

"Oh, all right. I'm sorry. I won't tease you anymore. We both get enough of that from our families."

Connie looked around and frowned. "Not meaning to talk shop, however, while you were out on Friday, I overheard someone talking about the Spivey case and said something about some additional evidence. Did Tim say anything to you?"

"No. I haven't heard from him since Thursday. I was going to give him a call today. He'll probably fill me in then."

"Good morning, Connie, Seth." Pastor Steve shook hands with both of us. "How's our patient doing?"

While Connie watched me with interest, I figured the less she knew, the better.

"It was a sprain. She's on crutches for a few weeks. When I went by this morning, she was in some pain but seemed okay."

"Good. I'll give her a call later this afternoon, let her know Sandra and I are thinking of her."

"She'll appreciate hearing from you."

As soon as Steve walked off, Connie turned to me, bursting at the seams with curiosity. "All right, give."

"There's nothing to give." I tried to act indifferent, but she wasn't buying it.

"Don't give me that. Who is this *she?* Do I know her?"

"I don't believe so." Again, I tried to look bored with the subject.

"Ah-ha. You can't fool me. There is someone, and you're keeping it a secret. Does Tim know?"

"There's nothing to know," I huffed out. Hopefully, she would take the hint I was finished with this conversation, but I had my doubts.

"I guess I could go ask Pastor Steve." She rested her elbow on her arm, tapping her finger on her chin.

"There's nothing to ask. After the wedding yesterday evening, Lori Morgan, Adam's sister, fell and hurt her ankle. I drove her to the clinic to keep Steve from having to take her. I felt it my duty to check in on her this morning before coming to church since I knew Steve would ask how she was doing. End of story."

She heaved out a breath. "Is that all? Well, phooey. For a minute there, I thought you'd finally found someone."

"Sorry to disappoint you. Now tell me more about the Spivey case. What did you hear?"

"They found additional evidence that might prove the husband's involvement."

Connie continued to explain what she'd overheard while I half-listened.

51

I didn't need her sticking her nose into my business or getting any ideas of playing matchmaker. There were enough people already playing cupid. I didn't need one more, especially where Lori was concerned.

Chapter 6

Lori

"Did your folks bring lunch?"

My heart raced at the sound of Seth's voice, so much so, I felt like fighting back to gain control over my emotions. I switched the phone to my other ear.

"What no preamble—how are you feeling? Are you in much pain? Isn't this a lovely day?"

"All right. How's this?"

His huff of breath brought me a smile of pure joy.

"Hi, Lori. I'm so sorry you are unable to enjoy the lovely weather we're having today. The temperature is a balmy 32 degrees, wind chill factor 22, which I believe would go a long way in cooling your feisty disposition. I do hope your ankle is feeling better. If not, may I come over and stomp on it to make it feel worse?" He breathed in. "How's that, Ms. Grouchy?"

Laughing, I choked out, "Well done, except maybe the stomping and grouchy part."

"I believe you asked for that."

Hearing the smile in his voice, I decided to concede. "You're right, I did. And to what do I owe this delightful call?"

"Just checking to make sure you've been fed properly."

"Sufficiently fed. Thank you for asking. My mom and Jim came by and brought Chicken Express which consisted of chicken tenders, mashed potatoes and cream gravy, green beans, rolls, and even a gallon of Blue Bell—Chocolate, my favorite."

"Well then. Would you like me to come by and polish off the Blue Bell for you? Can't have you lying around eating ice cream and getting fat."

My pulse raced at the thought of Seth dropping by for a second time today.

"I beg your pardon. I'm not lying around getting fat. It's hard work trying to move about my apartment while manipulating crutches." I breathed in knowing I sounded a bit *poor me.* "I have true respect for people who have to use these things as a permanent mode of transportation."

"I know what you mean."

"But if you'd like to come by and have a bowl of ice cream, feel free, there's plenty left. And just think, you'll be saving me from having to go to the fat farm."

He laughed. "I'm on my way. Should be there in five."

"Great." I was talking to thin air. Seth had already hung up. He probably did that quite often on people, or was it just me?

Scrambling off the couch, I did my hop-walk-clump to the restroom to make sure I still looked presentable. Why it mattered, I didn't know. My pride, probably. Certainly not to look good for Seth.

Barely through applying my lipstick, I heard a knock. I hobbled back into the front room and scarcely had time to get to the door when there was more insistent banging.

"Lori, it's me. Open up."

"I'm coming," I yelled. Yanking the door back, I scowled at the exasperating man. "You sure are short on patience." I looked up into the shocked face of a man I didn't know. "Oh, excuse me, I'm sorry."

My face flamed.

Seth stood behind the man laughing, which helped to fuel my embarrassment and temper all the more.

"Lori, this is my friend and partner at the precinct, Tim Baker. Tim, this is Lori Morgan, the invalid I was telling you about."

"I'm not an invalid." Still flustered and wondering why he had brought along a friend, I stared at Tim like he was some odd discovery before I remembered my manners.

"Nice to meet you, Tim. Please come in." I hobbled back, motioning them in from the hall.

The man was Seth's height and size, only this guy had rusty-colored hair, chocolate-colored eyes that sparkled, and a smile that would melt a spinster's heart. He was adorable and huggable, like a big, ol' soft teddy bear.

"Have a seat." I moved as gracefully as I could to the couch to sit down.

Seth was there beside me, taking my crutches, leaning them against the wall.

"Get your leg up."

"Pardon me?" I stared at him as if he'd lost his mind.

"Prop your ankle up on the pillow. It's supposed to be elevated. And where is your ice pack?" He looked around the apartment like a grouchy old man.

"In the freezer." I started to get up.

He pushed me back down. "No, you don't. Stay put. I'll get it for you." Grabbing the pillows, he stacked them and then reached for my leg. "But first, get that ankle up."

"Since when did you become my mother hen?" I cocked my brow, which Seth ignored.

Tim's chuckle drew my attention. Staring at us, he had a look of comical disbelief. Apparently, he found humor in Seth fussing over me. What Tim didn't know is Seth could hardly stand me. He just felt guilty for causing my injury.

"Put a sock in it, Baker, and make yourself useful. Get the ice pack while I get her leg propped up properly."

The teddy bear winked at me before doing Seth's bidding.

"Would you please behave and stop trying to impress your friend with how well you treat me. You and I both know the truth." I hissed. "And I can do this myself."

I jerked my leg around. Pain shot up from my ankle causing me to yelp.

"Now look what you've done. Probably injured your ankle more." Seth gently grabbed my leg, lifting it up on the pillows. He adjusted my ankle's position before stepping back satisfied. "There. Now doesn't that feel better?"

Through gritted teeth I said, "Yes. Thank you."

"Don't mention it, Princess."

"*Oooh!* Really?" I gave Seth a look of loathing, which he ignored.

"Here's the pack." Tim held out the blue gel pack, still smiling.

Seth again took charge, wrapping the frozen thing around my ankle.

He was right. My ankle was already beginning to feel better, but I wasn't about to tell him that little fact.

"Thank you." I directed my appreciation to Tim.

"You're welcome, Princess."

"Not you, too. I thought I would at least have an ally in you." I poked my thumb in Seth's direction. "He's bad enough. Call me Lori, please."

"Sorry. Lori, it is."

"If you're through kissing up to each other …"

Seth looked perturbed, which delighted me.

"I brought Tim by so that you could meet him. He's going to help ferry you around the times I can't. When you need something from the market or drugstore, or whatever, you'll call me, and either Tim or I will be by to take you or pick it up for you."

"As much as I appreciate your kind offer of help, if I remember correctly, I told you I wouldn't be needing your services." Seething inside, I tried for a pleasant expression but was afraid I missed the mark.

"I'm sorry Seth made you come all this way, Tim. However, my mother is going to be checking in on me. I won't need your help."

"I talked with your mother."

"You did? When?" To say I was shocked he'd spoken with my mother was an understatement. I was horrified.

"At lunch, and then just before I picked up Tim."

"Did you call her, or did she call you?" The three little lines between my brows tightened. I was going to give her one good piece of my mind as soon as Seth and Tim left.

"I called her. I wanted her to know she wouldn't have to worry about looking after you, unless she just felt she wanted to."

"Wow. Thanks." I snipped back, wishing I could do more to my self-imposed manager-of-affairs.

"No thanks necessary."

Tim chuckled, and I gave him a dirty look, which sobered him quick-like.

"Audrey said she'd be glad for the help. So you see, it's all taken care of." Seth rubbed his hands together. "Now, how about some ice cream."

Instead of telling him to go to the market and get his own Blue Bell, I bit my tongue. "I believe you know where the bowls are. Help yourself. But none for me."

While Seth set about the business of dipping up two generous helpings of ice cream, I figured it would be a hot day in January before I called Seth Singleton to help me with anything.

"How do you manage to keep sane, partnering with that guy?" I directed my question to Tim.

His laughter had me smiling. I liked this fellow.

"He's not so bad. In fact, I'm kind of used to him. I've known him since college. We've partnered together for over three years now. He's always had my back and I have his. That's why I'm here. When Seth asked if I'd help out, I figured I'd at least come and see what was so special and why he was so concerned about his sister's new sister-in-law. Now I know." He wiggled his brows at me. "The way I see it, taxi duty won't be half bad. In fact, I'm going to enjoy it."

I didn't like the fact that Seth was going to pawn me off on another guy, even if Tim did seem nice enough and willing. "Thank you, but I won't need your help."

"Don't spoil my fun. The way I see it, I'm helping a damsel in distress, which I'm going to enjoy."

Heaving a sigh, I said, "I give. You're as bad as Seth."

"Please don't compare me with this guy." He shot his thumb in Seth's direction. "I'm far more handsome, and my manners are impeccable. Where his are ... Well, let's just say, you'll find I'm a more likable fellow."

I liked Tim already, but I could tell I was going to have my hands full if he stayed around for long.

"Here, eat this before it gets all sappy, and you have to slurp it up instead of using a spoon."

Seth handed Tim a bowl piled high with chocolate ice cream that matched the bowl he carried in his other hand.

He pointed at Tim, "Don't let him fool you. This guy is a real lady's man. He'll feed you a line without a baited hook."

"And just when I was beginning to make inroads into Lori's heart." Tim winked at me.

"Inroads, my foot. She'll eat you alive and spit you out before you know what's happened."

58

"Really? That's what you think of me?" I couldn't believe Seth would think I was so cold-hearted.

"No, but I know this character. With your sharp wit, he won't stand a chance. And when you realize he's a lady's man, well, I'm just saying." Seth shrugged and shoveled ice cream into his mouth.

"Ahh, you do me a disservice." Tim glanced over at me. "Please don't let this guy taint your opinion of me. I'm a saint compared to him. Now Seth here, well I—"

"You were about to shut up and eat your ice cream." He gave Tim a pointed look.

"Yes, I was, wasn't I?" Tim saluted me with a raised spoonful and a silly grin. "I believe I will polish this off before it melts. By the way, Blue Bell is my favorite."

"Which can't be eaten while talking." Seth raised his brow.

"Point taken."

"I'll make sure I have plenty on hand for you when you come by." I smiled at Tim, ignoring Seth entirely.

Seth grunted, while Tim raised his brows. They both began devouring the ice cream in their bowls.

I was fascinated with their camaraderie. It was apparent they were close friends, almost like brothers. The thought of them dealing with unsavory characters had me a little unnerved. For some reason, I knew they loved being detectives.

They were handsome in their own right, but in my opinion, Seth was more appealing.

Tim, I liked, and knew he'd be an easy guy to be around, unlike Seth who thought it his mission in life to torment me.

If only he could keep from needling me, or trying to run my life like a pesky brother, he wouldn't be half bad. But if he truly treated me like he actually cared, I might get to like the guy *too* much.

Best keep it at sparring partners. So much safer, and a whole lot more fun ... *sometimes*.

Chapter 7

Seth

A small part of me envied how, right from the beginning, Tim and Lori had hit it off so easily. Come to think of it, a big part of me was downright envious. Putting the two of them together, outside of incurring Connie's wrath, had been a good idea, or at least, that's what I thought, at first.

Tim had successfully taken Lori off my hands. But here I sat second-guessing myself. What was the matter with me?

Maybe I shouldn't have foisted Lori off on Tim after all. What if they fell for one another? Would I be okay with that? And what about Connie? Didn't I owe her some loyalty as far as Tim was concerned?

The more I thought about the two of them together, the more their closeness ate at me. If I was completely honest, it wasn't because Connie would be hurt. It all boiled down to, I didn't want my best friend and Lori to like each other in that way.

With Tim's easygoing manners and southern charm, most women gravitated to him. And Lori seemed to be no exception.

Unlike with Tim, Lori and I got along more like sandpaper—abrasive, yet something good could be said about us. We seemed to smooth out each other's rough edges. *Or do we create more?*

I'd be the first to admit it was more my fault than hers. For some reason, it was just fun to push her buttons. I loved to see the sparks ignite her eyes, turning them a brilliant blue.

She always gave back as good as she got with her quick wit and feisty attitude, not to mention she was easy on the eyes. If it weren't for the fact that she was too likable and I was too susceptible to her lovely and somewhat prickly charms, I would enjoy dating her. But there was no way I was going to step into that caldron. I'd be boiled alive.

"What's up with Lori and you?"

Tim's intense stare had me wondering if I'd spoken my thoughts aloud.

"Nothing's up. Why do you ask?"

"I've never seen you this prickly over a woman before. Do you want to tell me what's going on, or do you want me to make an educated guess?"

"I repeat ... *there's nothing going on.* Lori is a quasi-relative I feel a certain responsibility for, especially since I was the one who caused her injury." I turned my attention back to the paperwork on my desk, not willing for Tim to ...what? See that I was interested in her?

"And since my time was tight, I was glad you had the time to step up and help me out. But, hey, if you'd rather not ..."

"No. I don't mind helping a beautiful damsel in distress. In fact, I've enjoyed our time together so far, doing whatever she needs, or taking her to dinner." Tim smiled, watching me closely. "Truth be told, I enjoy Lori's company. She's fascinating. She's talented, and to top it off, she's fun to be around. And I might add, we get along well."

Not liking how this conversation was going, I shoved my chair back, stood, tossing my pencil on the top of my desk.

"I don't know about you, but I think we need to do some real work. Are you ready to question the witnesses in the Huntley case? Or would you rather sit here and discuss Lori?"

"Man, she sure has you tied in knots." Tim chuckled, shaking his head. "But yeah, where do you want to start? The clerk or the woman who happened to see the suspect walk out of the store after it all went down?"

Still steamed over Lori apparently eating up all the attention Tim was showering on her, I didn't wait to see if Tim was coming. I snatched up my coat and headed out into the hallway, shooting over my shoulder, "You choose."

Walking at a rather fast clip, I jerked my suit coat on and then adjusted the collar and my tie. Without looking back, I could hear Tim close behind.

"Hey, wait up. We're not going to a fire."

I slowed my steps, knowing my anger with Tim was nothing short of jealousy and sheer stupidity. If it hadn't been for me, Tim wouldn't have met Lori.

Maybe it was time I took her off Tim's hands, at least for a few days. Perhaps even suggest he take Connie out on a real date. That would get Tim thinking in the right direction again. Being away from Lori for the last week and a half had mellowed my attraction some.

"Sorry, man. I have a lot on my mind."

"Namely a blonde with blue eyes and a sprained ankle?" He gave me a knowing look.

Hoping to draw Tim off the scent, I gave a hearty laugh. "Yeah, she's part of it but not in the way you think." I opened the door and slid into the driver's seat, pulling on the seatbelt.

Tim got in on the passenger side and began putting the address where we were going into the GPS.

I pulled out of the yard and made a right. "By the way, thanks for helping out with Lori. I can take over for the rest of the week."

"Believe me, it hasn't been a chore. As I believe I told you before, I've enjoyed her company." He glanced off smiling. "In fact, I don't mind finishing out the week. It'll give you more time to do whatever."

I should have been happy with his suggestion, even taken him up on it, but I wasn't on either count. For some reason, his words and confident smile grated against my nerves.

"No, I've imposed enough. I don't want Whitney coming home and finding out I left Lori in your care instead of helping her myself. My sister would never let me hear the end of it."

"If you're sure?"

"I am." Even if I weren't, I'd do the time. "Have you ever thought about asking Connie out?" I studied the carload of teenagers stopped next to us, acting as though they didn't have a care in the world. I couldn't remember being that carefree, but I'm sure I was.

"Not so sure that's a good idea."

"*Hmm*?" I glanced at Tim. "Oh, yeah, Connie. And why not?"

The teens didn't speed off like I thought they would, just took off slow and easy, making me happy I wouldn't have to stop and write them up.

"I like Connie. In fact, I would date her if I were prepared to make a commitment. But I'm not sure I'm ready. At least, not yet. You of all people should understand."

"I do." I felt the heavy weight of being alone.

We rode in silence the rest of the way until I pulled up in front of Mrs. Martin's house.

"I hope this woman's credible." Tim glanced at his notes.

"If her being the neighborhood watch means anything, we may have a reliable witness." I nodded in the direction of the house. The curtain was still moving from where she stood watching. I chuckled. "We'd better get up to the house before she calls the cops on us."

"I think your right."

Before we could knock on the door, Mrs. Martin had it open.

"May I help you?" She held a broom in her hand, more like a weapon.

Smart woman. Her astute observation of us had me grinning inside.

"Hi, I'm Detective Singleton, and this is my partner Detective Baker." I handed her my card, and Tim did the same.

"May I see your badges, please?"

"Yes, ma'am."

We produced our badges.

When she had thoroughly inspected both of our badges and our cards, she handed the badges back. She invited us into her living room, the same room I'd seen her watching us from the window while we sat in the car.

The woman was pleasant enough. Even sharp.

"Mrs. Martin, do you think you could pick out the man you saw running out of the store from a lineup?"

"Like they show on TV? A bunch of men in a little room behind one-way glass?"

Her eagerness had me suppressing my grin. "Yes, ma'am, but nothing as glamorous."

"Well, of course not." She scrunched her eyebrows together. "Those are TV sets, and the people are actors.

65

They don't lay their life on the line every day like the two of you do."

"Thank you. However, back to the man. If you saw him again, do you think you would recognize him?" Tim was doing his best to keep her on track.

"Yes, sir. Without a doubt." She smiled, causing her cheeks to shift upward, making the wrinkles around her eyes more pronounced.

"Would you be willing to come downtown and make a positive I.D.?" I hoped she'd say yes.

"I'd be happy to. Do you want me to come now?" She shifted forward on her chair, anxious to do her civic duty.

"We'd need a little time to set up a lineup. However, how about tomorrow? Could you come by then?"

"Certainly. What time?"

"Ten a.m." Tim picked up one of our cards she'd placed on the coffee table. He wrote the address and time on the back of the card and then handed it to her.

"Will both men be in the lineup? Or will you show them separately?"

"Both men?" I stared at her oddly before glancing at Tim. He shook his head. This was the first time we had heard about a second man.

"Yes. There were two of them. There was the one that did the shooting. The other one stood outside as the lookout."

Tim narrowed his gaze. "What makes you think this other man was a lookout?"

"Because when he saw the police car coming, he turned, looked inside the store, and then whistled. The young man didn't stay around. He hurried off in the opposite direction of the police cars." Mrs. Martin nodded, a confident look on her face.

"That was just a few moments before the other man, the one the police arrested, came running out of the store. He threw the gun in the trash barrel, and then took off in the same direction as the other one."

"Can you describe the second man?"

"Sure can. He was about your height, but skinny, like he didn't eat much." She motioned to me. "I couldn't see his hair because he had one of those black wool caps all of the kids wear nowadays, you know, even when it's hot out. It was pulled down around his ears and brows. He wore jeans with all those holes the kids like."

She tilted her head, plainly perturbed. "Can you believe they spend perfectly good money for jeans, then tear them up so they'll look that way?" She shook her head, her white curls bouncing. "Kids nowadays. I'll never understand them.

"Anyways, like I was saying, the young man had on a white T-shirt beneath one of those school jackets, orange panels and black sleeves. There was some kind of patch on the sleeve, but I was too far away to read what it said." She squinted in thought. "I believe I could pick him out if you've got him too, especially if he still wore that cap of his."

I finished writing down the description. "I'm afraid we don't have him in custody yet. But this will help."

"What a shame." She scrunched up her nose. Her lips puckered.

"Did you mention seeing this man to anyone else?" Tim was writing on his tablet.

"Yes, I told one of the uniformed police officers, but I didn't get his name."

"Would you mind looking through some photos while you're at the precinct tomorrow? Maybe you'll be able to spot him in one of them."

"Lands' sake, I wouldn't mind at all. I'd consider it my public duty."

67

"Thank you, Mrs. Martin, you've been most helpful." We stood. "We won't take up anymore of your time. But we look forward to seeing you tomorrow downtown."

Mrs. Martin followed us to the front door and then stood waving us off.

As soon as we got into the car, Tim punched in the address of the other witness released earlier from the hospital. "What do you think about the second man? Do you blieve he was the lookout?"

"It's worth looking into."

"I agree."

We fell silent. Our destination was the clerk who had suffered a superficial wound to her arm and was now on sick leave for a few days.

"Listen, I was just pulling your leg about Lori. Seeing if I could get a rise out of you." Tim smiled.

"Whatever."

"I like the woman, emphasis on *like,* nothing more."

I could feel Tim's stare.

"Listen, I may get in trouble here, but"—Tim rubbed the back of his neck, frowning—"I think you and Lori would be good for one another, and I don't mean as friends either."

"Not likely." I wasn't about to let him know I'd given some thought in that direction myself. He'd never let it ride.

"Why not?"

"She's practically family."

It was the only thing I could come up with at the moment, even if it did sound lame.

"Not by a long shot." He shook his head, smiling. "You wanna try and feed me another line?"

"Regardless what you think, I'm not getting hooked up with Lori. So drop it." I pulled up to the curb outside of our next stop, rather perturbed with my partner, hoping he'd take my advice and leave the subject of Lori alone.

"I'll drop it for now, but you haven't heard the last of this yet."

Chapter 8

Lori

"He's released me to go back to work on Monday." I hobbled my way over to where Mom sat in the doctor's waiting room.

She closed the dog-eared magazine and smiled. "Does that mean you can drive now?"

I wrinkled my nose. "No. He said not for another week. Will you or maybe Jim be able to take me to work and pick me up all next week?"

Mom rose from the chair, draping the strap of her purse over her shoulder. "I don't see where that will be a problem. Send me your schedule, and I'll put it on my calendar and in my phone."

We left the Doctor's office, heading toward Mom's car.

"What about Tim? Won't he want to pick you up some?"

"Mom! How many times do I have to tell you? Seth is the one who asked Tim to step in and help. And again I add, against my protests. I think Seth felt guilty my injury was partially his fault, but he probably didn't have the time to step in, so he asked Tim. Don't get me wrong, Tim's a great guy, but we're not attracted to one another. He's been doing me a favor, that's all. I've imposed upon him long enough."

"But he's so nice, and he seems to like you. Are you sure there isn't something more to it than he's just doing you a favor?"

I opened the door to the car and plopped down in the seat, allowing Mom to take my crutches and stick them in the back.

"*Yes, Mom,* I'm sure there's nothing between us. But I do have a new friend now, thanks to Seth. Still, I'm not about to ask Tim to take me to work or pick me up. He's already done enough. I'm not going to ask him to do more."

Mom slid behind the steering wheel smiling.

Giving her a stern look, I said, "And neither will you. Do I make myself clear?"

"Crystal." She backed out of the parking space before heading in the direction of my apartment.

"Mom, I'm serious. I don't want you calling Seth to ask him to help out. And don't you dare ask him for Tim's number. Do I make myself clear?" I gave her a narrowed-eyed stare, hoping she'd understand this was nonnegotiable. "If you or Jim can't take me, I'll call an Uber driver."

"Over my dead body." She became rigid.

I laughed.

"I find no humor in that, Lori. Just the other night in the news—"

"Mom, I'm kidding." I figured I'd better not press my luck. "I have a friend at work who will help out if you or Jim can't pick me up or take me."

"Oh? A friend?"

"*Yes, Mom.* Jackie. A woman at work."

Mom was worse than a bulldog. When she got something between her jaws it was next to impossible to

71

pry her teeth apart and make her let it go. And at the moment, it appeared a man for me was top on her list.

She pulled up to the curb in front of my building and stopped. "Are you sure you don't need help getting upstairs?"

"I'm sure. I've learned to maneuver quite nicely."

When she started to get out of the car, I said, "Stay put. I can get them." I leaned toward her, gave her a hug. "Thanks again for taking me to the doctor's office. I'll text you my work schedule when I get inside and settled."

I retrieved my crutches and waved her off before heading into the building.

When I reached the elevator, the doors opened. Seth nearly ran into me, knocking me off balance. I yelped and tried to right myself.

Seth reached out and steadied me. His quickness saved me from landing on the floor again and probably kept me from having another body part injured.

"What are you doing here?" I snapped at him, trying to hide the fact my heart was racing at the sight of him, not from my near fall.

"I was here checking on you. Where have you been? I've called your cellphone several times, but didn't get an answer."

"Oh, I forgot to take it off silent."

"Silent?"

"I was at the doctor's office and had my cellphone on silent."

"Why? Is there something wrong with your ankle?" Seth's brows puckered as he gave a quick glance down at my foot. When he saw nothing unusual, his glance slid all the way up my body, checking me out for defects, no doubt.

"I'm fine. The doctor wanted to take a look to make sure my ankle was healing properly before I go back to work. Nothing more." I looked at him oddly. "What are you doing here?"

Hearing someone clear their throat, I looked behind Seth and saw Tim standing there grinning.

How could I have missed seeing him? Seth, is why.

I smiled. "Hi Tim, I didn't see you."

"So I noticed." He winked at me. "It looks like you're getting around pretty good on those things."

"I am. In fact, I got a reprieve from the doctor just now, saying I could go back to work on Monday."

"All right."

Tim, at least, was excited. Seth didn't look so happy with my news.

"How will you be getting to work on an ankle that's still injured?" Seth looked like he'd eaten a green persimmon.

"My Mom will take me and pick me up."

"Depending on your schedule, I could probably help out some." Tim looked pleased with his offer.

"Thank you, but—"

"I live closer. I'll pick her up." Seth, looking bored, reached out and pushed the button for the elevator. "Right now you need to get upstairs and off that ankle."

"Like I said, I'm doing fine. In fact, I'm a whole lot better. It's practically healed."

Seth let loose a snort.

The elevator doors opened, and both men stepped aside giving me plenty of room to pass.

When Seth followed, I wasn't surprised. I figured they would come up for a few minutes.

When Tim followed, Seth gave him a sharp look.

"Didn't you have that little matter to take care of?"

At first, Tim gave him a puzzled look that cleared too quickly, accompanied by a silly grin. "Ah, thanks for reminding me. I sure do. And I'll take care of it right now."

73

Tim gazed at me. "I'll drop by another time to see how you're doing."

"I'd love that. Thanks, Tim. Bye." I gave him a huge smile then turned to Seth. "You needn't see me up. I'm more than capable of taking care of myself."

Seth pushed the close button, giving me an unnerving stare. "I can see that you are. However, I thought I'd come up for a while, hear what the doctor had to say."

"You needn't. My checkup went fine. And like I said, he released me to go back to work on Monday."

"That's good. But I'll need your schedule to make sure I pick you up on time."

His penetrating stare was beginning to unnerve me.

"That won't be necessary. My mother and Jim have agreed to be my taxi service."

"*Humph.*"

My insides were squirming under his intense stare.

The elevator stopped and the doors opened. I clomped-swung-hopped off the elevator. The rubber foot ended up between the hall and elevator floors, essentially getting stuck in the crack, curtailing my escape.

I chalked the accident up to being in the small confining space with Seth and his unnerving stare. Why he could make me so nervous when others didn't was a mystery.

Teetering on the brink of falling on my face or reinjuring my ankle, I felt Seth's strong arm around my waist. He held me up against him with one arm while pulling my crutch free with his other hand.

Before I knew what was happening, he took my crutches and leaned them against the hall wall.

"What do you think—" My breath was snatched from my lungs.

Seth had scooped me up in his arms against his rock-solid chest without so much as asking.

At first, speechless, I drew in a breath and then seethed. "Give me back my crutches and let me down. I can walk on my own."

"Yeah, and have you fall flat on your face? Not on my watch."

"No one asked for this to be your watch. And what about my crutches?" We were moving farther and farther from where he'd leaned them against the wall.

"I'll come back for them once I have you settled."

I huffed, crossing my arms, making my body rigid. "I won't waste my breath arguing with you. You wouldn't listen anyway."

"At least, you're getting smarter."

His sparkling brown eyes irritated me, yet at the same time turned my insides to jelly. One whiff of his faint woodsy cologne finished the job. I wanted to lean my head against his shoulder, close my eyes, and rub my hand across his scruffy beard. Would it be soft or tickle my palm?

What is the matter with me? When he's around I seem to forget all reasoning?

Simple answer? I was completely illogical where Seth was concerned. And though he was extremely appealing, I didn't want to have these thoughts about him.

Remember? Stubborn. Infuriating. Opinionated. Maddening. That's the Seth I know. So get your head on straight.

"Where's your key?"

"My what?" His face was too close to mine, jumbling my thoughts.

"Key. To your door. You do have one, don't you? Please don't tell me you leave your door unlocked."

"No, I don't leave my door unlocked. My key is in my purse. Which at the moment is dangling off my arm." I

75

pulled on the strap, bringing my purse up to my lap. "If you'll let me down, please."

"No can do. Not until you're on the couch resting with your leg propped up."

"*Oooh!*" I dug inside my purse, temper almost at a fevered pitch. "Has anyone ever told you that you are one frustrating, stubborn man?"

"I believe I've heard that a few times." His brow rose adoringly while his lips lifted into a cocky grin. "From you."

"I can't believe I'm the only one." I felt the rumble of his chuckle resonate through my body.

"Believe it or not, most women like me. I still can't figure why you are the exception to the rule."

"Well, let me count the ways …" I found the key and held it up. "Here it is."

He nodded toward the door. "Would you mind doing the honors? You're getting heavy."

Perturbed that he believed I was heavy, I said, "What? Are you a weakling or something? My mere 112 pounds shouldn't be anything for a man your size."

He leaned us down closer to the door so that I could insert the key. His cheek brushed mine. A shiver of pure pleasure rushed through me. I had finally found out. His beard wasn't as stickery as I thought it would be against my skin.

I looked at him. For a split second, it seemed the world stood still. His head moved closer to mine, blurring my vision. I could almost taste his lips.

The ding of the elevator broke the spell, shocking us back to reality. Though my hand shook, somehow I was able to insert the key and open the door to my apartment. But I couldn't look Seth in the eye.

"Are these yours, Lori?" Gregg Lambert, my neighbor from down the hall, stood by the elevator waving my crutches in his hands.

Heat flushed my cheeks again. For one of my neighbors to find me in Seth's arms made me over-the-top uncomfortable, even if it meant nothing.

"Yes, they are. I had a bit of an accident—ah-a near fall."

"Did you reinjure your ankle?" Gregg looked concerned.

"No. Ah ..." The words escaped me how to answer him.

"No worry. I'll bring them to you."

Seth practically dumped me on the couch and then started jerking pillows around to make a mound for my leg. I could tell he wasn't happy about Gregg. And not because Gregg found me in his arms either.

"Who is that guy?" Seth's brows scrunched together.

Fortunately, Seth's dark looks didn't scare me. "My neighbor, three doors down." I looked past Seth to Gregg entering my apartment. "Thanks, Gregg. You can set them here." I motioned to a place beside the couch.

"We'll discuss this later." Seth spoke under his breath before turning to Gregg. "Here, I'll take those." He practically ripped the crutches from Gregg's hands, and then leaned them exactly where I always placed them.

Oddly enough, he held out his hand to Gregg.

"I'm Seth Singleton, a *very* close friend of Lori's."

I wanted to speak up and say, *not all that close. In fact, we can't stand one another.* But I knew as far as I was concerned, that wasn't the truth.

"Nice to meet you." My neighbor smiled. "I'm Gregg Lambert. But I don't recall Lori ever mentioning you before." Gregg glanced back and forth between us, trying to puzzle out the mystery.

"My brother is married to his sister."

"Ah, now I get the connection. Family."

"Not even remotely connected." Seth's mouth was set in a straight line.

A huge grin spread across Gregg's face as he glanced back at me. "Would you like a cup of tea? I'm sure you're tired after the ordeal of seeing the doctor, and"—he glanced at Seth—"your near fall."

"That sounds great." I didn't attempt to point out where the tea things were. Gregg already knew.

Since he'd moved in, he and I had shared a few cups together. Gregg was pleasant enough. And once he understood he couldn't expect anything more than friendship or a cup of tea, he stopped asking me out on dates and became a good neighbor. He often came by to visit, sometimes bringing bakery goodies. Anytime Gregg had girlfriend woes, he'd drop by looking for a friendly ear to spill his troubles.

Seth watched him with heightened interest, more like Gregg was a suspect in a lineup or possibly a mosquito ready to suck out his last ounce of blood.

"How about you, Seth? Would you like a cup or were you leaving?"

"No. I'm staying." His words were more like a growl. "But no tea for me, thanks."

For some reason, I got the feeling Seth wouldn't leave before Gregg did.

I wonder if I could send them both packing?

Taking into consideration Seth's soured disposition, apparently brought about by Gregg, I decided it would be best to wait unless I wanted an altercation to break out in my apartment.

If one does, I wonder if I could ask them to take it out into the hall?

Chapter 9

Seth

Gregg being one of Lori's friends shouldn't have bothered me, but it did. His familiar behavior with Lori ate at my gut. Was he interested in her? Worse yet, was she interested in him?

What did it matter? We were just friends, if our many heated discussions could qualify us as such.

I settled into one of the overstuffed chairs, getting comfortable, willing to sit out this guy if I had to.

What did Lori know about Gregg? Probably nothing. Most women were too naive when it came to men. And she was probably no exception.

Once I left Lori's, the first order of business would be to do a background check on Gregg Lambert.

Watching Gregg carefully as he puttered around the kitchen, I did my best to size him up. The guy smiled too readily. *Smooth operator* came to mind. Come to think of it, he reminded me of someone with a mission—*Lori*.

"What line of work are you in, Gregg?"

"I'm in investments. Work mainly from my apartment."

"Investments, hmm. What? Stocks? Bonds?" I wasn't going to let him slide that easily.

"Yeah."

"Yeah? What does that mean?"

Gregg smiled. "I dabble a little in both. Boring stuff." He shrugged. "And what do you do?"

"I'm a police detective."

He looked me squarely in the face.

"I don't believe I've ever personally met a police detective. How long have you been on the force?"

"Three as a detective, five as a policeman."

Gregg studied me for several seconds, probably sizing me up as I was doing to him.

"Have you ever been shot?" Gregg's face twisted into a frown. "Sorry, I bet you get asked that a lot."

"Often enough. But in answer to your question, yes." A quick glance at Lori told me she was horrified. "Once."

Wearing a grimace, Gregg whistled. "Man. That must have hurt."

"It wasn't exactly fun. Hazards of the job and the criminals we encounter. It's something every officer figures will happen one day, but hopes and prays it won't. If an officer retires without getting shot at least once, he feels he's been fortunate."

The conversation was leaving a bitter taste in my mouth along with alarming Lori. "Are you going to drink that tea or give it to Lori."

"Oh, sorry." He handed her the cup.

"And what about you? Have you ever been arrested?"

At first, Gregg was taken aback, but recovered nicely. He gave a preposterous scoff. "Hardly."

He glanced at Lori. "Hey, I'm glad you're doing so well. But since you have one of Dallas's finest watching over you, I'll take my leave. I still have some work to do. And as always, if you need anything, you have my number. I'm just down the hall."

"Will do, and thanks, Gregg."

"Don't mention it."

80

I didn't like how she smiled at him. Nor did I like how he did a quick once over of Lori.

When the door shut, and she landed her sights on me, I knew I was in deep trouble.

"What in the world was that all about?"

She all but hissed the words at me. Her temper was blazing. So much so, I figured I'd get singed if I got too close.

"What do you mean?" I tried for innocent.

"Why would you ask Gregg if he had ever been arrested?"

I gave her a nonchalant shrug. "Curious is all."

"Curious, my foot. I—"

"Speaking of foot, how is your ankle doing?"

"Fine," she released on a huff. "But don't you dare change the subject." She took a couple of calming breaths.

"Hey, look, I was watching out for your interests here."

"Then stop. I don't need you, nor did I ask you, to look out for my interests. And furthermore, you have no right to ask Gregg such an outrageous question. He could have done a stint in Sing Sing, for all I care. It's none of your business." She crossed her arms, shaking her head.

"You *would* care if he came from Sing Sing."

"That's beside the point. I can well imagine you have few friends if that's what you ask when you meet them for the first time. It certainly isn't something a normal person would ask."

"Be careful. You're about to spill your tea. You'll get burnt." The *normal person* reference got under my skin … *a little*.

"We're not discussing my tea." Her cup clattered down on the end table, tea spilling over the rim onto the saucer as she huffed out her displeasure. "Why is it every time we're together you work doubly hard to try my patience?"

"How was I to know that you'd object to me asking a few questions? It didn't seem to bother him any." I smiled, trying my best to deflect her anger.

She rolled her eyes skyward. "*Ohh*, deliver me now."

Sitting quietly, I waited until she turned her attention to me again. "I apologize. Will you forgive me?"

For a few seconds, it was touch and go whether or not she would. She stared at me, no doubt weighing my sincerity.

Finally, she nodded. "Yes. Though I don't know why I should."

"Hey, listen, I'm not offering any excuses for my behavior. You need to understand something about me. One of the hazards of being a cop is possessing a fair amount of suspicious nature that surfaces at times. Especially when it deals with someone I care about."

If the display of her wrinkled brow meant anything, I figured she was having a problem believing my sincerity.

"Ask my sister, she'll tell you. Any guy who wanted to date Whitney underwent close scrutiny, not to mention a thorough background check of the guy ... including your brother."

"You've got to be kidding." Lori looked incredulous.

"No, ma'am, I'm as serious as a loaded gun."

"I believe you." She held up her hands in defeat, then dropped them back on her lap. "Wow! Even Adam?"

"Afraid so."

"That must have been something. Knowing my brother as I do, I bet that went over as well as a cop attending a criminals' convention."

I liked her sense of humor.

She sobered while watching me through narrowed eyes. "And what exactly did you mean by *someone I care about*? I didn't think we were all that close."

"We are, just by the nature of our acquaintance. I owe a certain responsibility to you, if for no other reason than you're my brother-in-law's sister."

"Well, please don't do me any favors. I don't need you to do a background check on any of my friends. I hope that's clear enough for you."

"It's clear. No can do. It's too late."

"What's too late?" She looked cute with her puckered brow and scrunched up nose.

Before I could close my mouth, I said. "I have no choice. I already care about you, and not because we're semi-related."

Chapter 10

Lori

I was past being shocked. Seth's *care about you* didn't mean attracted to or interested in, even if my feelings and sentiments were beginning to waiver in that regard to him.

His *caring* was more like he watched out for family. Somehow, to his way of thinking, that included me.

"Have you eaten dinner?" Seth drummed his fingers on the end of the armrests.

I stared at him, trying to figure him out. He was a puzzle, and the more I knew about him the more I liked him, even if he did aggravate me ninety-nine percent of the time.

Though I wanted to hold on to my anger, I couldn't. Teasing the guy was more fun. And if I got a rise out of him, more the better.

"No. Is that an invite as in *let's go out*?"

My question seemed to fluster him, but he recovered nicely with a sweet grin.

"Invite, yes. Date, no. I'm hungry and figured you might be too. So are you or aren't you—hungry, that is."

"I'm starving."

"All right, then what will it be? Go to a restaurant, or take out? Your choice."

"I'm all for staying put. And Chinese, please. That is if you like Chinese."

"Sounds good. What do you want to order?"

I thought for a moment. "I'll have one vegetable roll, egg drop soup, sesame chicken with noodles, oh, and lots of fortune cookies."

He gave me an incredulous look. "Is that all?"

A gurgle of laughter erupted. "Yes. What are you having?"

"Since it doesn't sound like you'll be sharing, I'll order beef broccoli."

"*Ooo*, that's good too. I might have a bite or two of yours." I swung my legs off the pillow onto the floor.

"Just where do you think you're going?"

"I'm going to get my money."

"Afraid not. Your money's no good. I'm buying."

"You don't need to pay for mine."

"Yes, I do. I asked you to have dinner with me, remember?"

"Oh. Well, I-ah want to get out of these clothes and into something comfortable, which I'll do while you're ordering our food."

Seth held out his hands.

"I can walk on my own."

He let out an exasperated sigh. "You can, but I was going to help you stand."

"Oh, sorry." I reached up. "Thanks."

The warm clasp of his hands gave a jolt of pleasure I didn't expect. When he pulled me up, I overcompensated, teetering off balance. He grabbed me around my waist to keep me from falling, his cheek brushing mine.

His scruffy beard barely grazed me. Desire soared through me as heat flooded my face. Standing crushed up against his solid chest, loving how it felt, I realized I hadn't made any effort to move away.

Coming to my senses, I overreacted. I pushed away from him, once again teetering and then falling back on the couch. Only this time, Seth followed me.

My breath whooshed out as he landed on top of me. Looking into his eyes, his breath mingling with mine. I was as confused as he appeared be.

Perplexed with the chaotic feeling running amuck inside me, I pushed him. Annoyed with myself for being unable to control my emotions, I overreacted once again. "Would you get off me?"

He scrambled to stand up. "Did I hurt you?"

I shook my head, too affected by emotions to answer.

Before I knew what he was about, he had me around the waist, standing, crutches under my arms, and brushing my hair out of my face.

"Stop that. I can do it myself." I slapped his hand away before shoving the remaining strands of hair behind my ear.

Motioning him away, I said, "Order the food. I'm going to change clothes."

"Yes, ma'am." His puzzled stare was once again unnerving.

Turning abruptly, I hopped-clumped out of the living room into my bedroom, shutting the door with a little more force than I meant to do. Slumping back against the door, I relived the last excruciating minutes of humiliation.

How would I ever face him without turning red?

"Lori?"

I nearly jumped out of my skin. By the sound of his voice, he was standing right outside my door. I waited to answer until I had moved farther into my room, clearing my throat. "Yes?"

"Are you decent."

"Why?"

"I don't want to leave until you're ready to lock the door behind me."

86

"Give me a couple of minutes." I rushed around, slinging off my clothes, pulling on my old, comfy warm-ups. After giving a quick look in the mirror to ensure I didn't look like something out of one of Lucille Ball's madcap adventures, I hobbled to the door and then crutched my way into the living room. Seth was half-sitting on the bar stool glancing at his phone.

I cleared my throat. "You can go now."

Instead, he stood there looking me over. "Wow! When you said *get into something comfortable*, you meant it."

Now I wished I'd rethought my choice of comfy. My ratty warm-ups were okay for me but not quite up to snuff for company. "I-I—"

"I'll be back in about ten minutes."

Seth was out the door without giving me a chance to defend my choice.

Before I could hobble over to the entry, the door opened, and Seth stuck his head in the room.

"You are going to lock this, right?"

"If you remember, I'm operating more like a turtle than a roadrunner. I'm on my way."

He winked and smiled. "Take your time. I'm not going anywhere until I hear the lock tumble into place."

"Oh, for Pete's sake. Leave, will you."

"I heard that. And I don't know who Pete is, but I'm not doing this for his sake but yours."

I laughed while making a big production of locking the door.

"I'll be back soon."

For some reason, Seth's concern for my safety made me feel warm inside, like I was cherished.

With my emotions all scrambled and running high, I decided to make our dinner fun. I shoved cushions on the floor on one side of the coffee table, making the front edge of the couch a backrest. I pulled out a couple of red placemats and black napkins, along with two pairs of chopsticks, and a fork, just in case Seth didn't know how to use chopsticks.

At the last minute, I grabbed the colorful Chinese lantern I'd saved from my college days and another pair of chopsticks. I placed the paper lantern on the table over a small tea light.

I ran my fingers through my hair, pulling it back away from my face and twisted it up on my head before securing it with the two chopsticks. Since I didn't have a kimono, my comfy sweats would have to do. I wasn't trying to impress Seth after all.

Pouring the boiling water into the teapot, I heard a tap on the door and Seth calling my name.

When I finally unlocked the door, Seth breezed in, stopped and stared, and then whistled.

"Hey. You've gone all out." He gave me a look of appreciation then saw my sweats. "Well, almost." Shrugging, he laughed. "There is something to be said about being comfortable, I guess."

"Especially with my bum ankle." Embarrassed, I wished I'd changed.

"There is that."

He slipped off his shoes, shoving them under the counter, and then proceeded to pull the paper containers with little metal handles from the paper bag. He placed them on the coffee table, and then unceremoniously dumped a bag full of fortune cookies all over the table and placemats.

"Oh, good." I rescued one from the floor and began tearing at the wrapper. "I'm glad you didn't let them scrimp on the cookies. They're the best part of the meal. Before dinner." I popped a piece in my mouth, closing my eyes while savoring the cookie's crunchy goodness. "*Yum!* And after."

"Now that I know those little cookies can turn you sweet, I'll make sure I have a bag of them with me at all times."

I threw one at him, which he caught easily with one hand.

"Don't be ugly. It's not becoming." I finished off the other half before reading my fortune.

"What does it say?" He nodded at the little slip I held in my hand.

"Choose wisely. Your choice will bring you happiness." I chuckled. "And that's what I'm about to do. Now let's see what we have in each of these little perfumed boxes of delight."

"Perfumed?" He wrinkled his nose. "Did I go to the right place?" He grinned.

"Yes, at the moment, this food smells better than any perfume you can buy over the counter."

He chuckled, shaking his head, then looked at me inquiringly. "Plates?"

"Huh? Oh, yeah. In that cupboard." I pointed. "I guess you don't like eating out of the cartons?"

"Cartons are okay. But I figured since you went to all the trouble of setting the stage, plates or bowls would be nicer."

The heavenly aromas mingled in the air, causing my stomach to clench tightly with anticipation. Or was the upheaval I felt caused by being here alone with Seth in such an intimate setting?

I pushed the thought back into a dark little place in my mind to pull out later when I was alone and had time to examine my feeling concerning him.

By the time he got back from the kitchen, I was sitting on one of the cushions, my emotions well in hand, opening containers.

"This is like Christmas all over again."

He gave me an odd look. "How so?"

I giggled. "Wow, even you are getting in the mood.

Again, he looked at me oddly.

"*How so ...*"

"Ha. Ha." He rolled his eyes.

"Okay. The boxes. Since I can't read the chicken scratch on the flaps, I have to open it to see what delicious surprise awaits me inside. *Mmm.*" I closed my eyes, breathing in deeply after opening one.

When I looked up, I found Seth, his head cocked to one side, staring at me with a funny little grin in place. His expression was difficult to read and made me feel awkward. "What? Don't you like surprises?"

"Yeah, who doesn't? However, watching you open those boxes gives a whole new meaning to surprise. I've never seen anyone get so thrilled over food boxes. You must be starving."

"Yeah, there is that, but ..." I purposely looked at the table not wanting Seth to see my chagrin at what he must think as my child-like behavior.

He came around and sat down beside me and began helping me open the remaining boxes.

"I see what you mean. There is some enjoyment opening a box when you're not sure what you'll find."

"Hang with me, and I'll have you dancing in the rain." I slumped inside.

Why can't I keep my big mouth shut?

"I'm not sure that will ever happen. I don't dance, and I don't care much about standing out in the rain and getting all wet."

"Party-pooper."

He shrugged, his stare unnerving me.

When all the boxes were open, I held out the container with the soup.

"I think we will need some bowls unless you want to eat out of the same carton."

He rose. "What? And have you eat my half because it was on the bottom. No way. I'll get the bowls. I want my fair share."

By the time he made his way back to our quasi-table, I had myself under control, or I prayed I did.

After eating the soup and egg rolls, I spooned out noodles and rice onto my plate.

"Hey, no fair, unless I can do the same." He gave me a challenging look.

"What?" I looked at him innocently.

"You took some of my fried rice."

Giving a majestic wave of my hand over the boxes, I said, "Help yourself. I'm not stingy." I sat back and watched him load his plate with fried rice, noodles, and then proceeded to unload some beef broccoli and orange sesame chicken on top of the pile.

I gave him the same challenging look he'd given me earlier, adding the hike of one brow.

He proceeded to scoop out chicken onto one side of my plate, then beef broccoli on the other, topping off the middle with a small patty of egg foo young smothered in rich mushroom sauce.

"Ooh, I didn't see that. I love egg foo young."

"I'm glad I could please you. That can be difficult at times."

Not certain if he was teasing or serious, I decided to ignore it and eat.

For the next few minutes, all was quiet while he and I stuffed our mouths. I was in bliss, every bite a burst of flavor that I couldn't help but enjoy wholeheartedly.

Beginning to get full, I wiped my mouth and watched Seth continue to scarf down the food on his plate. The man certainly knew how to enjoy a meal and had quite an appetite.

He caught me watching and gave a puzzled look. "What? Do I have sauce on my face?" He wiped his mouth while watching me.

I shook my head. Heat rose up my throat. No doubt, my cheeks would soon be turning ten shades of bright pink.

"I'm stuffed." Shoving my plate back, I folded my hands over my full belly. "And I don't have room for another bite."

"Not even for one of these?" He held up a fortune cookie.

Snatching it from his hand, I said, "There's always room for these little gems."

Seth got up and started clearing our table.

"Leave it. I can deal with it later."

"No. You stay put. I'll put the leftovers in the fridge."

While he worked in the kitchen, I moved the cushions back on the couch and sat down, feeling guilty that he was doing all the clean up.

"Are you sure you feel up to going back to work on Monday?"

His concern was touching.

"Yes. My ankle is much better. Almost like new. I just have to be careful not to apply too much pressure on it. Otherwise, it's fine. And … I'm getting bored. And then there's that little thing called a salary to keep a roof over my head."

"If money's what's motivating your return to work, I'd be more than willing to help you out. That way, your ankle will be stronger, and less likely to reinjure it."

He came into the living room, grabbed the pillows, and much to my protest, propped my leg up.

"Are you training for a new career?" I adjusted my leg, a little peeved that he was hovering, yet loving his attention.

"No. Why?" He gave me a strange look as he sat down at the end of the sofa, my foot precariously close to his face.

"I just figured you were in training to become a nurse, or maybe a mom." I waved at him and my leg.

"Ha-ha. Funny." His lips formed a straight line. "No, I figured your ankle should be elevated. But I'm sure you will do as you please."

Feeling awful over my ugly behavior, I said, "Sorry. I appreciate your concern. But I can do with a little less attention if that's okay with you."

"In other words, *back off?*"

"*Welll* ..." I smiled to lessen the blow.

He nodded. "I get the message." He looked around the apartment then back at me. "Since it's getting late and you've been properly fed, it seems my services are no longer needed. I have some work to do at home and also an early morning, so I'd best be shoving off."

Seth stood. "But I'll come by around noon and bring you lunch. How does that sound?"

"You don't need to. If you remember, I have leftovers aplenty." I motioned to the kitchen.

"I'll see you tomorrow night, then. Dress casual. I'll take you to dinner and a movie."

"Seth, what's going on?" I looked at him oddly, more than overjoyed we would spend time together and not be sniping at each other.

"What do you mean?"

"First you sic Tim on me, and now you're here acting nursemaid. The accident wasn't your fault any more than mine. There's no need for you to pay penance. I'm okay.

And as far as I'm concerned, you've done far more than was necessary."

"How does a guy go about asking you out on a date without you turning it into a federal case?"

"Is that what you're doing? Asking me out on a date?"

"Yes." He shuffled his feet, acting out of his depth.

"This isn't payback for a supposed wrong?" I slipped my feet to the floor.

Seth held out my crutches.

The mere brush of his hand brought excitement.

"Thanks. But I only need one crutch." I handed the second one back to him. "Well, which is it. Payback or an honest to goodness, bona fide date?"

"Let's just call it a friendly date. I thought you might want to get out of the apartment and see a movie after being stuck here for the last couple of weeks."

"I do, and I will—accept your *friendly* invitation." I hoped the action on his part leaned more to attraction than obligation. But, hey, this was Seth, the guy who loved to get a rise out of me. I'd take what I could get.

"What time?"

"How about six. That'll give us enough time to eat and then take in a movie." He moved to leave.

When he opened the door, he stopped and turned abruptly, nearly bumping into me. I started to topple over backward once again. Around him, that was becoming the norm.

Grabbing my waist, he steadied me but continued to hold on. His face was close enough that I could see the tiny specks of gold in the dark brown of his eyes. That is, until he lowered their gaze to my lips.

I drew my lower lip through my teeth, as my heart thumped loud and hard, nearly beating out of my chest. I wondered if he could feel the pounding. Would he know how his touch had affected me? I prayed he wouldn't.

What I was feeling would get me into trouble, especially with Seth. I wanted more, so much more. But did he?

Seth cleared his throat, dropped his hands to his side, and then looked everywhere but at me.

"I was going to say, you pick out a movie you would like to see, and I'll choose the restaurant. How does that sound?"

"Sure." I raised my brows and gave him a huge, silly grin.

"Why does your smile provoke an uneasy feeling inside me?" He smacked his forehead with his palm. "Oh, I get it. A chick flick of the worse kind."

He shook his head. "Growing up with my two sisters, I had to endure a ton of chick flick movies. I'll show you I can be the better man and suffer through any chick flick you throw my way. But"—he wiggled his eyebrows up and down—"next time, I'll pick out the movie, you the restaurant."

"So there will be a next time?" I looked at him challengingly.

"See you tomorrow night. Make sure you bolt the door. And maybe you should still use two crutches."

He had completely ignored my question.

I didn't press him. Instead I said, "Yes, sir." Unable to snap my heels together, I gave him a salute along with a cheeky grin. "But no to the second crutch."

"You're impossible." He closed the door chuckling.

I waited to see if he would leave before I locked the door. I didn't hear any movement.

"Lori, the lock."

Just for the fun of it, I waited a few more seconds, and then finally drove the bolt home. Only then did I hear Seth walk away.

95

Taking a deep breath, I leaned against the wall. Where the warmth of Seth's touch had been, a chill seeped in making me cold and lonely.

Seth's worry over my safety made me feel special and wanted, even if his concern came from an ingrained habit learned from family and job. I also knew if he had any notion I was taking his worry for my safety in a romantic way, he'd set me straight, right quick and proper.

That's all right. A gal could dream, couldn't she?

It was a definite ... I would be hard-pressed to dream of a better man than Seth.

Chapter 11

Seth

"How's our patient doing?" Tim watched me from his desk, a smug smile riding his lips.

"*Our* patient is fine. Or at least, she was last night when I left." I wasn't going to play Tim's game of a hundred questions. Nor was I going to allow him to probe into my private life. Though we knew almost everything there was to know about each other, there were some things that were sacred.

Lori was one.

"I need you to find out all there is about this guy." I threw the sheet of information I had gathered on Gregg across the desk at Tim. "I'll do a background check while you see what else you can find out about him?"

"Hmm. Is this Gregg Lambert, the guy that lives in Lori's building?"

"One and the same." I stared at Tim. "What do you know about him?"

Tim shrugged, his face screwed up with disinterest. "Nothing much. Seems like a good neighbor. Helps Lori out some. Other than that, nothing. Why?"

"I don't know. I have an odd feeling about him. And I don't like how he looks at Lori when she's not watching."

"Oh-ho! Do I sense a spark of jealousy?"

"Not at all." I shook my head trying my best to act natural. "He just comes across like a smooth operator. And he was evasive when I asked him if he'd been in jail."

"*Whoa!* I bet that went over like seeing a process server."

I laughed. "She wasn't too happy." I sat down and made a note on my computer. "But when you have some time, check the guy out for me, will you."

"Sure. As long as I'm best man at the wedding."

Wadding up a piece of paper, I threw it at Tim's head. "Anymore talk like that, and I'll be looking for another partner to ride shotgun." I picked up a file. "Now what's up with the Huntley case? Do we have any leads on the other guy?"

While glancing over the page of notes, my mind didn't retain anything I read. All I could think about was one gorgeous blonde who was too trusting.

Tim looked at a message on his desk. "Mrs. Martin called and said she saw that same guy, who was standing outside the store, walking across the street from her house." He glanced up from his note. "I think the guy must live somewhere close by. Otherwise, why was he on her street?"

"You've got a point. Let's drop by Mrs. Martin's and see if she remembers anything else or if she's seen the suspect again."

"Sounds good." Tim stood, pulling on his coat while following me out to the car.

"Are you going to check on Lori tonight or shall I?"

We were half way to Mrs. Martin's when Tim sprung his question and for the same reason as earlier, it didn't set any better with me.

"You won't need to. I've got it covered." I could feel Tim's curious gaze pinned on me.

"Look, I don't mind if you'd rather have some more free time. Lori and I get along well together. In fact, I enjoy being around her. I think she'd be a nice person to date and see where it goes."

I wanted to tell Tim to back off. If Lori dated anyone, it would be me. But instead, I said, "If you want to date her, then by all means, ask her out. As far as she and I are concerned there are no strings attached." I made a right turn onto Mrs. Martin's street. "You know my philosophy about me and dating."

"Sure do, but I think you'd be crazy to let a woman like Lori get away. You won't find another one like her in a million years. And if I'm reading your vibes correctly, and I believe I am, I think there's a whole lot more than *like* involved."

"If I did like her in the way you suppose, I wouldn't act upon my feelings. So drop the subject."

"Okay, man, but I'm just saying ..."

"Enough about Lori." My words came out harsher than intended, but Tim took the hint and got quiet.

We pulled up to the curb and by the time we were halfway up Mrs. Martin's walk, she had the door open, greeting us.

"I didn't expect to see you so soon again." She waved us inside the house. "Come on in and sit a spell."

We followed her into the living room.

"We would like to talk with you about what you reported yesterday."

"You mean the young man who stood as lookout?" Her eyes snapped with excitement.

"Yes, ma'am." Tim glanced down at his notes. "Would you mind telling us again where you last saw him?"

"Why, certainly. I was getting the mail out of my mailbox when I heard someone whistle. I thought I recognized the sound right off as familiar. When I looked around for the source, this guy was walking away. He disappeared around the corner." She pointed to the north. "I'm sure it was the same young man. And it stands to reason he lives around here somewhere, since the little market is less than two blocks away."

I stood. "Thank you for your help, Mrs. Martin. Detective Baker and I will do some canvassing in the neighborhood and see if anyone recognizes the man from the sketch artist rendering."

She followed us to the door and opened it, allowing us to pass through, then came out and stood on her porch. "I hope you find him. I'd feel a whole lot safer if you do. Just the idea he might be right next door, doesn't make for pleasant thoughts."

"We'll do our best to apprehend him as quickly as possible. In the meantime, if you see him again, don't confront him. You have our card. Call us."

"I certainly will."

"You have a nice day, ma'am." I nodded in her direction.

"You do the same."

She stood on the porch waiting for us to drive off, or, at least, that's what I thought she was doing, until she started quick-stepping it in our direction, frantically waving at us.

"Hold on. Mrs. Martin wants something." Tim rolled down his window.

She came charging at us as if a rabid dog was chasing her.

"That's him." She hissed, nodding in the direction of the corner.

A young man was walking in our direction on the other side of the street.

"You sure?" Tim unfastened his seatbelt.

I did the same, already reaching for the door handle.

"Yes, I'm sure. That's him. And he's wearing the same jacket he wore the day of the robbery."

"Mrs. Martin, go back into the house, shut and lock your door. We'll take it from here."

"All right." She gave another quick glance in the man's direction then hurried back inside.

While Tim alerted dispatch, I got out and crossed the street, walking toward him. When he saw me coming, he looked around, spotted our car, then glanced at me again. Before I could tell him to stop and put his hand up, he turned and made a run for it in the opposite direction.

I yelled, identifying myself as an officer, and told him to stop and put his hands up.

Instead, the suspect kept running.

Motioning for Tim to take the car and go around the block to head the suspect off, I followed after the man. He had torn off down an alley, already out of sight.

I cut across the grass and followed the suspect into a dead end alley lined with tall concrete block fences with driveways leading into attached garages. The young man had reached the far end, trapped, looking around for a way to escape.

With only one way out, which I was blocking, he'd have to scale one of the concrete fences, or find a garage open for easy access to a house. Otherwise, he'd have to come through me, meaning I had my man.

Seeing me, he made an attempt to scale the wall, but couldn't get enough traction.

I pulled my gun from my holster and advanced on him, yelling, "I'm Police Detective Singleton. Stop right there and put your hands in the air."

When he landed on his feet, he turned and drew a gun and aimed it at me. The suspect was no older than eighteen or twenty, at best. He had the wild look of a caged animal.

I skidded to a stop. "Listen, man, you don't want to do that. If you shoot me, you'll go up for murdering a cop. So why don't you put the gun down and let's talk."

He gave a quick shake of his head, narrowing his gaze.

An ingrained reaction had me pulling the trigger at the precise moment I witnessed his finger move. The muzzle flash and a simultaneous blast from his gun filled the alley. A searing pain ripped through my chest, throwing me back against the concrete wall. The impact had me momentarily stunned.

Hearing another round of fire, I tried to gain my footing, but couldn't move. Moments later, I heard someone running toward me. I reached out for my gun that wasn't there.

Sounds came and went, while the pain burned in my chest.

"Hang in there, Seth, I'm calling for a bus." Tim rattled off our position.

"The boy ..." Though I tried, I couldn't lift my head to look.

"Don't worry about him. He's been subdued. Stay still."

He rolled me slightly on my side. The pain, excruciating. I tried not to cry out but a groan escaped.

"I'm making a pack for your back." He rolled me back over and began pressing on my chest with his palms.

"What are you doing? Trying to kill me?"

"No. I'm doing my best to keep you from bleeding out."

Tim's words were fading.

"Don't close your eyes. Stay with me, Seth."

The sirens were getting closer. Though I tried to concentrate on Tim's voice and do what he said, I couldn't. My eyelids were heavy and breathing difficult.

"I'm afraid I can't. Tell Lori ..."

***

The pain in my chest wouldn't stop nor would my head quit pounding. I tried swallowing, but couldn't. My tongue stuck to the roof of my mouth and felt drier than a Texas creek bed in August.

In the distance, I heard people talking, but my efforts to focus were useless. Everything seemed light years away, yet, so close. I tried to latch onto the dream of Lori smiling, holding her arms out to me, but the awful ache in my chest snatched it away.

"Get the nurse. He's coming around."

"Mom?" I opened my eyes, trying to focus. Everything was hazy, and then mom came into view. That's when it all came back to me.

I'd been shot by that kid. But what about Tim? Was he all right?

"I'm here, dear." Mom patted my hand. "How are you feeling?"

"Like I've been hit by a freight train." I tried to smile, not sure I accomplished one though. My voice was scratchy and rougher than an old rusty bucket.

"I wouldn't doubt it, but at least, you're all right. That's the main thing."

Someone coming into the room snagged mom's attention. "Oh, good. Here comes your nurse."

She released my hand and moved back away from my bed.

A woman wearing pink scrubs, smiled at me. "Hi, I'm Pam. I'll be your nurse this evening." She ran a thermometer over my forehead. A blood pressure sleeve tightened around my bicep until I thought it was going to cut off the circulation

"Can you tell me, from one to ten, what your level of pain is?"

"One being?" *How does one measure pain?*

"One hardly any pain. Ten being unbearable."

"Then I'd say it's good enough to rate about a seven." I attempted a smile. "Would there be any way I could talk you into getting me some water. I feel like my mouth is full of cotton."

"I can give you a sip of water with your pills. And then some ice chips to suck on for now. Other than that, you'll have to wait at least another hour or so before I can give you more."

She held out some pills giving me an explanation for each of them. Then she gave me a small cup with hardly any water in the thing. The water barely got the pills down, but didn't come anywhere near quenching my thirst.

After handing me a cup of ice chips, she moved to her computer cart. When she was through entering her data, she pushed her cart to the door.

"The doctor will be here shortly. However, if you need anything—"

"Yeah, I know the drill." I held up the device that connected me to the nurses' station and the world outside my window, the TV.

Dropping it on the mattress, I grappled with a few ice chips, allowing them to melt in my mouth. Even if the chips didn't compare to drinking a full glass of water, it helped some.

Mom moved over next to me again, bringing Dad with her this time.

"Hello, son. How do you really feel?"

"Not too bad, considering." I glanced around the room. For the first time since waking, fear gripped hold of me. "How about Tim? Is he okay?"

"Tim's fine. He stayed until you got out of recovery and into the room. Said he had to go to the station and fill out the report, but he'd be back later to see how you're doing."

"The suspect, what happened to him?"

"As far as I'm concerned, he got better than he deserved after shooting you." Dad shook his head. "They have him at Parkland with two gunshot wounds."

"I only remember getting off one shot."

"Tim shot him the second time when he tried to pick up the gun again and shoot you. He's fortunate to be alive." Dad looked disgusted. "Apparently, he was high on drugs. That's why your shot put him down but didn't keep him down."

"Thanks." Feeling the effects of the pain pill, I began to drift off. My heart filled with pity knowing the young man wouldn't stand a chance where he was heading.

Chapter 12

Lori

Seven. I was steaming. Seth said six o'clock. The least he could have done was give me a call and say he wasn't coming or would be late, instead of leaving me hanging.

But no. He couldn't be bothered. The man was a detestable, stinkin', rotten bum in need of a truckload of manners in how to treat a woman.

I hobbled over to the refrigerator my temper turning worse.

Robbie raised his head from his bed watching me.

"It looks like I'll be staying home with you. Seth's a no-show, so I'm not going anywhere." I opened the door to the refrigerator and peered in like something good would magically jump out at me.

If I hadn't been such a pig at lunch by finishing off the Chinese leftovers, I could have eaten that. My only excuse, getting around on a bum ankle requires a lot of energy.

Who was I fooling?

A knock on the door had me closing the refrigerator. I headed to the entry, ready to give Seth a good piece of my mind.

Robbie jumped out of his bed and followed me barking.

"You have my permission to take a hunk out of his leg."

Robbie twisted his head and gave me a curious look as I continued to hobble toward the door.

"Hold that thought. Maybe I should hear what he has to say for himself before you bite him. But it better be good. If it isn't, I'll give Mr. Seth Singleton a good piece of my mind, and then you can take a chunk out of his leg."

Robbie did a little dance and barked again.

I swung open the door. "Well, what happened—"

My cheeks burned. It wasn't Seth. It was Tim.

He sent his friend to tell me he'd changed his mind. What a coward.

"Hi, Tim, come on in."

Robbie pranced around his friend, no doubt thinking Tim would take him for a walk like he normally did when he came to check up on me.

I brandished my hand about, motioning Tim into the room, while trying to give him a welcoming smile. I missed the mark by a long shot.

Tim reached down and picked up Robbie, snuggling him in his arms, rubbing the top of his head, before setting him back down on the floor.

Robbie looked at both of us curiously, then pranced back to his bed.

"I came by to let you know Seth won't be able to make your dinner date."

"Oh, really?" Making a big production of looking at my watch, I said. "I believe I figured that one out for myself a little over an hour ago. Come on in and sit down."

I hobbled over to the sofa, feeling the sting of Seth's defection. "Don't tell me he sent you to do his dirty work."

"No. Not exactly. Seth couldn't make it. I hope you won't be too disappointed, but I'm afraid you're stuck with me as your dinner partner, if that's all right."

"Sure. I like your company much better." I smiled, knowing I was speaking a lie. Oh, sure, I didn't spar with

107

Tim, and he was nothing like Seth. But somehow, Tim didn't quite match up to his partner. "At least, we don't see who can take the first jab."

"There is that." Tim moved to sit down.

There were tired and haggard lines in his face, a side of Tim I hadn't seen before.

"A busy day at the office?"

He looked down at his hands. "Yeah, you could say that. It's been a rough one."

Letting out a heavy breath, he glanced up. "I was asked not to tell you, but I think you should know." He rubbed his chin, grimacing. "Besides, you'll find out soon enough."

"Know what?" When he was slow to answer, my stomach knotted. I gripped my hands until they hurt. "Now you have me worried. What's wrong? Has something happened to Seth?"

He nodded. "Yes, he was shot today."

"Seth? Shot?" My heart stopped. I couldn't catch my breath. "Is he ... Did they ..."

Tim shook his head reaching out to hold my hand. "No, no. He's in the hospital."

I clung to his hand as I gulped a deep breath. My heart kicked in, racing like a greyhound on one of those little oval tracks.

Fearing the worst, I had to ask. "He's okay, isn't he?"

I wanted assurances, yet, an eternity came and went as I waited for Tim's answer.

"Yeah, they got him patched up, and he seems to be doing okay. He took a bullet in his chest, but thankfully, it didn't strike any vital organs. It was a through and through. He'll be in the hospital for a couple of days."

"Who told you not to say anything to me?"

"Seth."

I hurt deep inside when Tim told me Seth was shot, but nothing like now. My heart went cold, and my spirit was crushed.

So this is how it feels to love someone who doesn't love you in return?

Swiping at the tears that were on the brink of falling, I chewed on my bottom lip to gain control of my emotions. I wondered why Seth didn't want to see me, when I needed to see him in the worse way.

"Which hospital is he in?"

"Baylor."

"I would like to see him, that is, if he can have visitors." I paused, barely getting the words out. "Even if he doesn't want to see me."

"It wasn't that he didn't *want* to see you, exactly."

"Don't make excuses for him, Tim, even if he is your friend."

"I'm not making an excuse. It's just, he didn't want you to worry." Tim raised his brow. "I'm not sure he'll be happy with me for bringing you to the hospital."

"It's either you take me, or I drive myself. Your choice." I showed him a stubborn set to my jaw.

"I'll take you because I believe seeing you will do him a world of good."

"Since I'm already dressed for dinner and a movie, we can go now." I needed to see with my own eyes that Seth was alive and doing well, and then I would leave and not come back unless he asked me to.

The thoughts of him suffering tore me up inside, even if he did cause me no amount of grief on a daily basis.

Tim stood. "Where's your coat? It's cold outside."

"In the closet." I got off the sofa, grabbed my one crutch before hobbling to the laundry room. "In Robbie, come on, boy."

He obeyed like a little trouper.

"Good boy." I gave him a scruffy pat on his head and then pulled down a new rawhide and a biscuit treat from the cupboard. After ensuring his water bowl was full, I pulled the doggie gate closed. "You be a good boy. I'll be back soon.

Captivated with his treat, Robbie ignored me completely.

Tim held out my coat while I slipped my arms inside. "You seem to be doing a whole lot better since I saw you yesterday. One crutch, no less."

"I'll be glad when I don't have to use any and I'm walking on my own."

By the time we were in the car heading to Baylor, my insides were a quivery mess. Knowing how men trivialize most things, I had a truckload of worries eating at my gut. Mainly, Seth wasn't doing as well as Tim had said. And ... what if he told me to leave?

Well, I can be just as stubborn.

I glanced out the side window. The knot in my throat stung as I silently prayed Seth would be all right.

Tim stopped outside the entrance to the hospital.

"You go on inside. I'll park and be with you in a few minutes."

I did as told and entered Baylor, looking for a place out of the way to wait for Tim.

"Lori?"

Turning toward the voice, I smiled when I saw Addie and Don stepping off the elevator heading in my direction.

"I thought that was you. I'm so glad you came to see Seth. He'll be so pleased."

She hugged me and then Don gave me a hug too. "We just left him. He's on the 8th floor. Room 8015. You can go on up."

"Oh, I'm waiting for Tim. He's parking the car. When he gets here, we'll go up together."

At first, I saw regret in Addie's gaze, but she recovered quickly and smiled.

"That's nice. I know Seth will be happy to see you both. I was going to stay the night, but he wouldn't let me. Men." She shook her head. "Seth's in some pain, but they're controlling it with meds. He's in and out. But I'm sure he'll be happy for your company."

"Addie, Don." Tim walked up and embraced Seth's parents like old friends. "How's he doing?"

"Better." She waved at me. "As I was telling Lori, he wouldn't let me stay. Shooed us out of the room. Told us to go home. But whether he likes it or not, I'll be here in the morning once his father's off to work."

"Well, we won't hold you any longer." Don put his arm around Addie. "Have a good evening."

When we entered Seth's room, it was dark with only a single night-light at the entrance, giving shadows to the room. We moved closer to his bed. His silent, helpless form, made me want to cry.

A flicker of pain crossed his face. I grabbed the bed railing to keep from reaching out to touch his brow. I felt any show of concern coming from me wouldn't be welcomed.

He was hooked up to an I.V. drip, one with clear liquids and one with what looked like blood. The monitor displaying his vital signs bleeped across the screen and looked healthy. But what did I know?

I watched as he struggled for breath—his chest rose and fell so slightly it scared me.

Seth opened his eyes, smiled at me, and then closed them. In a flash, his eyelids opened again looking at me as if he couldn't believe what he saw. His brow wrinkled.

"Lori?"

"Yes, I'm here." I reached out and clasped his hand.

111

His fingers were icy cold, but they closed around mine, holding on.

"How are you feeling? Are you in much pain?"

"No. How did you get here?"

"Tim brought me. Are you cold?" It concerned me that his hand was like ice.

"A little."

Looking around for another blanket, I started to go check.

He held tight. "No. Don't go."

I looked at Tim. "Could you see if there is a blanket in the closet. If not, would you mind asking the nurse.

Seth looked past me. "Tim?"

"Yeah, I'm here, partner." He stepped up next to me, gazing down at Seth.

Seth blinked several times, and then as if he remembered what he'd forgotten, he let go of my hand.

"I thought I told you—"

"I know what you said, but I thought Lori had a right to know."

"Why would you keep something like this from me?" I gave Seth a stern look, the same I would give one of my errant students.

As a teacher, I didn't tolerate any sass or deception, and I certainly wouldn't tolerate Seth hiding things from me, or tearing into Tim for doing what he thought was right.

"It's fortunate for you that Tim told me you were here. If I'd found out after you had been released, you would be back in here in short order."

When he didn't understand my meaning, I said, "You'd be recovering from injuries you received from me for being so foolishly pigheaded."

Seth chuckled then grimaced, holding his chest. "*Man*, it hurts to laugh."

"Good. Fitting retribution for trying to keep me away." I propped my hands on my hips. "I would have found out tomorrow when Adam and Whitney came home. And how do you think that would make me feel. Like I didn't matter, is how."

"That's right, they're flying in tomorrow."

"Yes, and I plan on letting your sister know just how you treat your friends. Appalling."

Seeing that Tim was still in the room, I asked, "Would you check for blankets? Seth's cold."

"Sorry." Tim's eyes were sparkling with laughter. "I'll go check."

I could tell Tim was being highly entertained by Seth and me. But I didn't care. Seth wasn't going to treat me like someone who didn't matter. And the quicker he understood that fact, the better, regardless if he was recuperating from a gunshot wound, especially after last night.

I believed we had turned the corner in our relationship. Hopefully, that wasn't a pipedream.

Tim left the room, and I turned to face Seth again.

"Listen, Lori, I'm sorry. But I figured once I was released from the hospital, I'd give you a call."

"Yeah, and how would that make me feel? Like road kill, is how."

He started to chuckle but stopped and grabbed hold his chest again.

"After last night, I thought we had something more between us than mere sparring partners. But apparently not." I hobbled over by the windows, sliding the blinds back. Thinking to see one of the other Baylor complexes, the window gave a view of the Dallas night skyline.

"Lori."

I turned to find Seth's haunted eyes staring at me. His brow wrinkled in concern.

113

Hobbling back to his bed, I rested my hands on the top bar of the rail. I glanced down at the man who had become dearer to me than I could have ever imagined. My gaze roamed over his face, stopping at his eyes, eyes filled with sadness, pleading for my understanding.

He turned his hand over, palm up, extending it to me as far as he could reach.

I clasped his hand allowing his cold fingers to tighten over mine.

"I didn't want to care for you. And I certainly didn't want you caring for me." His words were soft but emphatic.

His saddened expression was tearing my heart apart.

"Well, that's too bad. We don't often get what we want in life, do we?"

"How true."

He rubbed his thumb across the back of my hand, the sensation warming my heart.

"From the start, I knew you were different. I couldn't keep my distance. Last night proved it."

"Seth, listen to me. If you're worried I don't feel the same, I do. When Tim told me you were shot, it felt like my heart was being ripped from my chest. I thought I had lost you."

"I'm sorry for causing you pain. I ..." His voice trailed off. He loosened his grip and closed his eyes.

Why was he so reluctant to share his feelings with me?

"They gave me a hot blanket." Tim came walking through the door. "This should warm him up in no time." Tim shook the blanket open over Seth's still form.

Reaching across Seth, I grabbed one end as Tim grabbed the other. We pulled it up over him, but he didn't move.

"His meds must have kicked in." Tim watched Seth for a few seconds then turned to me. "Since you haven't had dinner yet, and I haven't either, would you like to go to this little family-run Italian place close by? They have really great food. We can come back after dinner."

Tucking the blanket up around Seth's shoulder, I nodded. "Sure. Sounds good."

I laid my hand against Seth's cheek, feeling the warmth of his face, the scruffy bristles tickling my palm. From the first, I hadn't wanted to care about Seth, but now it appeared I had no choice

I moved around to where Tim stood, gave Seth one last look before walking out the door. My heart was heavier than when I had walked into the place, which was illogical since Seth was doing well.

For whatever reason, he was fighting the attraction that we both felt. And I, for one, wanted to know why. I wouldn't press him for the answer tonight or even for the next couple of days, but once he felt better, we would have that talk. And for once, he wouldn't squirm his way out of giving me answers.

Chapter 13

Seth

The moment Lori walked out of the room with Tim, I wanted to call her back—tell her not to leave. But I couldn't. The fact I was in here in the first place, was good enough reason to let her go.

I would steer clear of her and those beautiful blues eyes that could stare into my soul and see *way* too much.

Though it made the pain in my chest almost unbearable, I pushed the button to raise my bed to look out the window at the Dallas skyline.

I could still see Lori, her back to me, unaware I watched, while I stored up memories for my starved soul. Her profile, with that little turned up nose, the stubborn set of her jaw, even worrying her bottom lip as she was so prone to do, would give any dying man the will to live.

Her beauty wasn't outward appearance only. She was beautiful on the inside too. Kind, warm-hearted, and generous to a fault, the woman was also as tenacious as a pit bulldog.

Lori could hold her own in a verbal sparring match, probably due to those little rug-rats she taught at school. And no matter how hard I tried, I couldn't stop from loving her.

Disgusted that I couldn't control my emotions any better than I was doing, I lowered the bed into a more comfortable position and closed my eyes again.

Lori, with worry etched deep into her face, played upon my mind. I knew I couldn't let her know how I felt about her. She deserved better than what I had to offer. She needed a man who would bathe her in love, instead of showering her with worries.

The first—love—I could do unconditionally and without hesitation for the rest of my life. But it wouldn't be enough. Like today, the second one—worry—would slowly creep in, smothering out the love until she became a shell filled with nothing but heartache and regret. I wouldn't let that happen to Lori.

I didn't want her visiting me in the hospital, or like my Aunt Rachel had to do with Uncle Dale, visiting me in the morgue.

A chill wracked my body. I pulled the blanket up beneath my chin.

The soft, subtle smell of cologne—sweet but sexier than all get out, but was *so* Lori, filled my senses. The ache in my chest from the bullet was nothing compared to the pain I felt knowing I loved Lori but could never tell her. I wouldn't allow myself to experience her love. And ... I had every intention of driving her away.

Just as I'd feigned sleep to get Lori to leave tonight, I'd do whatever it took to make her forget me.

My night nurse strolled into the room pushing the computer cart. She went through the routine of running the thermometer, checking and entering my vitals into the computer, and all her other duties.

"Your company didn't stay long."

She handed me pills and a glass of water with a straw.

"They went to eat."

"None of my business, but is she your girlfriend?"

117

I nearly spit the pills I had just put in my mouth, across the room. I gulped a breath, grabbing my chest that hurt like it would explode, then hastily took the drink of water.

"Are you okay?" Pam looked ready to come to my rescue.

I waved her off. "No, I'm good. Just swallowed a pill the wrong way." I took another drink then set the Baylor logoed plastic drink cup on the table. "Tim and Lori are friends."

"Ah." Pam moved around adjusting my I.V., adding another bag of clear liquid and then taking down the empty one that had held blood.

"Are you in much pain?"

"Some, but bearable." My other pain wasn't something she could fix.

"Better to stay on top of it. Would you like another pain pill?"

"No, I'll be fine." I wanted to ask her if she had anything I could take for heartache, but I already knew the answer and what I had to do.

Cut off any and all ties with Lori. Be friendly, but not overly. Treat her like I did my kid sister. Keep my distance.

Yeah, and while I'm at it, cut out my heart and stick it on a spike. I wouldn't need it any longer.

The nurse left, and I closed my eyes, wishing the pain of loving Lori would go away.

Not sure how long I slept, or even if I had, I smelled Lori's sweet perfume. I breathed in deeply, then opened my eyes. Lori was next to my bed staring down at me.

I turned to look at the window and then at the clock. I hadn't slept through the night, and Lori had only been gone a little over an hour.

"What brings you back?"

"Before we left to eat, I talked with one of the nurses. She said you didn't get out of surgery early enough to have dinner, but you could have something now. So I figured I'd remedy the problem."

"Where's Tim?"

"He'll be here soon. He dropped me off, and he's parking the car. I came up with your dinner in case you were awake and starving."

"Did you go for Italian?"

She raised her brow, grinning. "So you *were* faking it."

"Busted." I couldn't keep from smiling. Lori was too adorable and *too* smart.

"I told Tim you weren't asleep. Whether it's because he's a faithful friend or because he's someone who can't recognize the signs of "faking it,"—she held up her fingers making the double quotes sign—"he assured me you were out for the count."

"I gave it a try." My gaze roamed over her face, storing up memories for later.

"I can't be fooled that easily. After handling over 150 kids a day for the last four years, I've run up against some of the best. And your small fake doesn't compare to the real live fakers I deal with on a daily basis."

A smug smile appeared. "Face it, Detective Singleton, you can't get rid of me that easily. You've met your match."

Unable to resist, I patted the side of my bed. "Come here, you."

I'd figured tonight, I'd give in. Tomorrow I'd be more up to speed.

She rolled the table over by my bed before moving up next to me. Again, I held out my hand, needing to touch her, feel her warmth. Not because I was cold, but because I couldn't resist her love, if love was what she was offering.

My fingers slid around hers, loving the feel of her hand in mine, and knowing I had fallen hard for this sassy schoolteacher.

Tomorrow, when I am stronger, I'll resist her. Tonight, I need her too much. I want to feel her love.

"Seth, what's happening?"

"What do you mean?"

"There you go again, fakin' it. I can see right through your phony act." She smiled, then sobered.

I started to protest, but she waved me silent.

"Whether it's love or fascination, I don't know. It's too soon. But this attraction between us is more than friendship. It's much deeper."

"Lori," I released my breath. "If you can wait until I'm home and feeling better, we can have this conversation. However, right now, I'm not up to having it tonight." I closed my eyes, feeling exhausted and weak. This time I wasn't *faking it*.

"I'll wait. But in the meantime, I won't allow you to shut me out of your life."

"Is our patient eating dinner?" Tim walked in smiling.

Lori released my hand and moved back and started pushing the rolling table over my bed.

"No, but he will be." Opening a sack, she tore it down the sides, making a placemat out of it. "Do you want me to feed you, or can you sit up and feed yourself?"

The smell of something good was making my mouth water.

"I'm a grown man. I think I can handle it." I pushed the button on the bed, doing my best not to grimace as it moved my back higher in a quasi-sitting position. My chest was on fire making it near impossible to tolerate food or anything else for that matter.

Lori hobbled around to the other side of the bed, took command of the control, and lowered me some.

"That should alleviate some of the pain and make it so you can tolerate a little food." She placed a napkin under my chin and across my chest. "And that will keep the nurse from having to change your lovely gown."

She got a cute little teasing look in her eyes. "Is that thing really open in the back so that you expose your backside to the world?"

I growled, "Yes."

"Well, how nice." She chuckled while taking off the lid to the container. "Now, whether you like it or not, I'm going to help you. So don't fight me, because this time you'll lose."

She could be headstrong at times, even stubborn, but I'd never seen her this determined.

After opening the Styrofoam bowl, she unwrapped a plastic spoon. "The nurse said to keep it on the lighter side, so I figured chicken noodle soup from Chick-fil-a would be light but hearty enough for a man's appetite."

She moved a spoonful of soup to my mouth.

"I'm not sure how hot this is, so be careful."

"I can feed ..."

"Take the bite, *please*." She raised a brow.

"I believe you better do what the lady says." Tim was grinning like he was thoroughly enjoying himself.

Lori was unmovable. She patiently held the spoon out in front of me.

I opened my mouth, feeling foolish. However, the first bite was so good I continued to cooperate.

"Have you heard what's happening with our suspect?" I addressed my question to Tim, trying my best to divert my attention away from Lori. My gaze kept straying back to her though. Apparently my will had a mind of its own.

"I checked while I was out. They have him in a room cuffed to his bed. He'll be there for a few days, but he'll live." Tim was plainly disgusted. "In my opinion, much better than he deserved."

"That may be." I wiped my mouth. "But he'll get due process of law. And if all goes well, do some hard time."

A grunt came from Lori. "For what he did to you, he should be locked away for good. Here take another bite."

Again the spoon hovered close to my mouth. I felt like an overgrown baby, but also, knew Lori was unmovable. So without protest, I allowed her to continue to feed me.

Tim kept up a steady stream of talk.

Lori willingly added her two cents.

I interacted little. My mind was occupied analyzing all the emotions Lori could provoke in me.

One thing for sure, I knew I wanted her in the worst way. However, after this stint in the hospital, I wasn't about to act upon my feelings or test the waters to see how far things between us could go.

Chapter 14

Lori

For two days, Tim picked me up and dropped me off at the hospital. And for two days Seth did his best to ignore me. Though I worked hard to break through his resistance, I found it impossible.

Something had changed in him overnight.

Oh, he was friendly enough. We talked about anything and everything, but nothing that really mattered. Nothing was mentioned of how we felt about each other or where we'd go from here. We were no closer now than we were before the shooting, which surprised me.

I would have thought, even hoped the hospital experience would have opened his eyes. Maybe create in him a desire to reevaluate his life's choices and hopefully realize he loved me. But nothing.

His near-death experience had sure made a change in me.

After Friday night, what I thought was a good start for getting closer with Seth, Saturday and Sunday were like Friday night never happened. He never once asked to hold my hand or even acted like he cared I was there. Other than I was someone to keep away the boredom, I could have just as well stayed home and wished I had.

On the first day, I made one attempt to touch him. He quickly removed his hand and placed it on his chest.

As plain as day, without words, he told me he didn't want me to touch him. I would have kicked him in the shin for his snub right then and there if I didn't have a bum ankle and he wasn't laid up in a hospital bed recovering from a bullet wound.

I went home and in the privacy of my apartment, cradled Robbie in my arms and cried all over his doggie hair. He took it like a trouper, even licked my cheek once as I told him just how despicable Seth was and how I didn't like the man. And how I wasn't going back to see the jerk again.

My resolve lasted until the next morning when I called Tim and asked if he'd give me a ride up to the hospital before church.

Tim did. He dropped me off in front of the hospital and said he was going for breakfast, and would come pick me up later.

When I walked in smiling, I was met with much the same as I received on Saturday. Once again, Seth acted like I was an unwanted guest.

This time, after about five minutes, he turned on the TV and became engrossed in a program, ignoring me completely.

I figured I could wait it out and, fortunately, ten minutes later, I received a text from Tim saying he was parked out in front of the lobby, to come down when I was ready.

His mother walked in and found her son ignoring me and scolded him for his poor manners. But instead of apologizing, he made it clear I needn't visit again. And since he would be released that afternoon and staying at his parents' home for a few of days, it might be best if he didn't have visitors so he could get some rest. *But thanks for coming.*

Sure, you're welcome ... not.

On the ride to church, I tried to act cheerful. All during the service and even on the ride home, I placed a smile on my face, acting cheerful. It was difficult keeping my emotions in check and acting as if life was good when all the while I was dying inside.

When I finally reached my apartment, I was spent from being on the visible stage all morning. I grabbed up Robbie and boohooed into his soft coat, while my little companion commiserated by whining along with me.

Once I stopped obsessing over Seth, I pulled out my class books and began working on my lesson plan. I went a whole hour without thinking about the man.

Today, I was determined more than ever I would forget about Seth. He would have to contact me if he ever wanted to see me again. I wasn't going to put myself out there for him to trample on my feelings.

If he was fighting his attraction for me, I was at the point of not caring. I wasn't going to wait around for him to figure out what he wanted, or even if he cared.

After putting on the finishing touches of my makeup, I scrunched handfuls of my hair in my hands, glad that this wasn't one of those wild, bad hair days. Thankfully, my hair fell nicely around my shoulders and down my back without turning into frizz.

Smiling, I thought of the children in my classroom. It would be wonderful to be back teaching my eager foreign students who were excited to learn. Most of the children were like little hungry birds, impatient for the next little word morsel they could try on their tongue, even if they couldn't pronounce it quite right the first couple of times.

At least, while working, the kids would help me forget about ...

I glanced at the clock and raced into the living room. *Well,* let's just say I hurried as fast as my clop-step-clop-step would take me.

"I'm going back to work today, Robbie. So you will need to be a good boy. Into your room."

His black eyes snapped with anticipation as he danced around my legs. When I paid him no mind, he headed off to the laundry room.

"Good boy." I gave him a good rub and then patted him on the head. "You be good, and when I get home, we'll take a walk in the park. How does that sound?"

Robbie barked enthusiastically, looking hopeful.

I made sure he had his toys before digging into his treat box and pulling out a biscuit. "Sit."

When he did, I gave him his treat. "That's a good boy. See you tonight."

By the time I got downstairs and to the front, my mom was there waiting.

"Are you sure you're up to this?"

"Yes, Mom. If I stayed home another day, I'd go stir-crazy. Especially since I can't drive for at least another week." I glanced out at the street. Though it was only six-thirty, the morning rush traffic was in full force. "Thanks for picking me up. I know how driving in this mess can be a nightmare."

"I'm just glad I can do something for you for a change. Jim said he would drive you tomorrow. I think he wants some father-daughter time."

"Great! I could use some time with him too." I wanted so badly to open up to Mom, needing a warm, sympathetic shoulder to cry on. But I knew if I told her how I felt about Seth and how he had treated me the last couple of days, she'd be all up in arms.

Maybe if I told Jim, he would have an answer. That is if I got up the nerve to broach the subject.

"Addie said Seth came home yesterday." Mom had her little matchmaker grin in place.

My heart sped up, not sure where she was headed with this conversation. I knew I didn't want any of part of her surmising and fixing Seth and me up.

"She thought it was awfully nice of you to visit him in the hospital every day."

"Hmm." *Yeah, and did she tell you how he trampled on my feelings and practically told me to leave the hospital?* I bit my lower lip to hold the words in, near tears.

"Addie mentioned he seemed in low spirits. She hoped you would come by to see him maybe today or tomorrow. If he saw you, she believed it might cheer him up." Mom gave a quick glance in my direction. "We could stop by on our way home this afternoon. What do you think?"

I wanted to scream *drop it, would you please.* Instead, I said, "I'm afraid I'll be too tired, especially since this is my first day back. It's always grueling with the kids not yet settled down from the Christmas holidays. And with them having a sub all last week, no telling how they'll be. After walking around and dangling my ankle from a chair all day, I'm sure I'll be exhausted."

Feeling her stare, I kept my face averted from her probing eyes, doing my best to feign disinterest in the subject.

"Maybe I'll drop by this morning and see how he's doing."

"That'll be nice."

"I'll let you know how he's feeling when I pick you up."

"Sure. Whatever. How are Adam and Whitney doing? Did they enjoy their honeymoon?" I figured this would get Mom off the scent of Seth for a while, or at least until she dropped me off at school and said goodbye.

Enthusiastic about her new daughter-in-law, she told me all about their Hawaiian honeymoon, and how they both sported a bronze tan.

I was never happier to see the approach to the school drive than this morning. She barely got stopped before I was opening the door.

"Thanks, Mom. I'll see you around four-thirty."

"Would you like me to tell Seth anything?"

Yeah, good riddance. "No, I can't think of anything." I shut the door and hobbled to the back door, grabbing my crutch. More than happy to make my escape, I waved her off.

I limped into the hall at my school and headed for the front office. Kathy was there, tickled to see me. She gave me my messages and some of the scuttlebutt of what I missed over the last week. Everyone who passed me said *glad to have you back.*

At least, I was wanted and loved here at Wilder Elementary.

In all my classes, the kids were super good and seemed overjoyed to see me. I didn't even have a problem out of Hikima, the little boy who, at times, could be a bit troublesome and hard to handle.

By the time school let out, I was ready to go home. For real, I was exhausted, but in a good way. I hobbled out to the front hoping to see mom's car but found Tim instead.

I opened the door and peered inside. "Did my mom send you?"

Tim's smile was refreshing. "Nope, I volunteered. I've gotten used to picking you up and taking you places."

His chuckle warmed me, causing me to smile. "Good. I was bolstering my psyche for another twenty minutes of inquisition from my mother. I'm glad it's you instead."

"If you'd like, I could do the inquisition."

"Don't you dare." I slipped into the car and gave him a big grin. "Home, James. Or in your case, home, Tim."

"Yes, ma'am." He pulled away from the school. "Would you like some dinner? My treat."

I released a heavy breath, grimacing. "I'm afraid I can't. I promised Robbie a romp in the park. And that little fellow has a memory like a pygmy elephant. And then I've got a lot of teacher catch-up to do."

"All right. Then why don't I take Robbie to the park, then when we're done, I'll call for takeout. How does that sound?"

"Better than a cup of soup. I accept, as long as it's a fully-loaded pizza."

"Hey, a girl after my own heart."

"I don't think I'm the girl that has captured your heart. I believe there's a Connie somewhere out there in your future."

"*Oh-ho*. Who's been talking to you? Seth?"

Just the mention of his name deflated my good spirits.

"Nope. You're the one who has mentioned Connie, several times in fact. And I've noticed when you talk about her, you have a certain sparkle in your eyes and a sound to your voice. I can see there's something special about the lady. And then yesterday at church, I knew I was correct. You only had eyes for her." I raised my brow, tilting my head to one side watching him. "You know I'm right."

He shrugged, his loveable grin in place.

"Hey, I know it's not my place to speak, but I wouldn't waste time, if I were you. You may wake up and find Connie's heart is elsewhere because of the lack of interest you've shown."

He pulled up to the front entrance of my apartment. I opened the door and was on the verge of getting out of the car when Tim touched my arm.

129

"Thanks for your advice, Lori. I believe I'll follow it. I don't want Connie getting away."

"Smart man. So, why in the world, are you sitting here with me? Give the girl a call. I can fend for myself. Believe it or not, I can call for pizza delivery as easily as you."

He gave me a comical look. "Really. Are you sure?"

"Positive." I slipped out of the car and opened the back door to retrieve my crutch. "Don't waste another minute, Detective Baker. Go get your man, or in this case, call and ask your lady out. Believe me, you'll thank me for it later."

"Thanks, Lori. I owe you one."

"You sure do. One night soon, I'll expect you to bring Connie and a fully-loaded pizza to my apartment, ya hear?"

"It's a date, if she'll have me."

"She will."

His lips tightened. "Man, Seth doesn't know what he's losing by being so stubborn."

"Later, friend." Stinging inside, I let the Seth comment slide and waved him off.

Overjoyed for my friend, I was glad that one of us could have that *at-the-top-of-the-hill* moment. I walked inside, my heart breaking, wishing I could get my hands on Seth and shake some sense into his head.

You've got that right, Tim. Seth doesn't know what he's lost.

Chapter 15

Seth

Home over two weeks, yet not one word from Lori. Addie, her mother, had visited the two days I was at the folks, but she never mentioned Lori or even if Lori had said *hi,* or even inquired about me.

So much for women.

No, so much for Lori.

Thankfully, Tim dropped by almost every day, catching me up on the cases. Surprisingly, he never once broached the subject of Lori, and I wasn't about to ask.

Before the shooting, it was *Lori this, Lori that.* Now it was *Connie this, Connie that,* until I was sick of hearing her name. All he sang were the praises of Connie.

What was wrong with me? I've never been this grouchy before. I'm usually easy going. Now it seems all I can do is gripe and complain. Probably, because I've been cooped up for two weeks and know I'll be on leave for another two weeks. Even then, all I had to look forward to was a desk job for at least a couple more weeks, which didn't appeal to me at all.

Thankfully, I'd been released to drive, as long as I was careful. Otherwise, my buddies would be locking me up with the rest of the criminals. I snatched up my keys and headed out the door.

My cars occupied the two-car garage. My black Jeep was great for off road and around town. My sweet ride was the car I inherited from my grandfather. A black 1978 two-door, Ford Mustang II King Cobra with gold racing stripes and all original parts.

The Mustang was one car I felt sure my neighbors could do without. But having a cop in their neighborhood outweighed the occasional annoying sound of the Cobra's loud pipes.

My house, though smaller and older than most, was purchased because of the cul-de-sac and the view out the back windows of the wilderness park. The neighbors were friendly and liked having a police detective on their street. Probably made them feel safer.

I got into the Mustang, pushed the garage door opener, and then revved up the motor. A couple of pumps on the gas and the sound of the *varoom-varoom* had my spirits soaring. Backing out, I waved at Mr. Barker, my next-door neighbor who was picking up his mail. I backed around and headed out of the cul-de-sac.

Not knowing where I was heading, I got on Highway 75 going toward downtown, thinking to head east and out of the city. When I reached the Woodall Rodgers short stretch of freeway, I steered my car up the on-ramp without thinking. Veering off the first exit, I angled around to where Lori lived on Routh Avenue.

I pulled into the first free parking space, turned off the engine, and then sat staring at Lori's apartment window.

*What was I doing he*re?

I knew. I had to see Lori. Find out why she hadn't stopped by to see me or, at the very least, called. Apparently, she didn't care if I were living or dead. I needed to know why ...

Shaking my head, I knew the answer. I had all but run her off with my rude behavior.

Shame and remorse settled down around me and had me reaching to turn on the ignition. Hearing a knock on my car window, I turned to see who it was.

I looked up into the beautiful but stormy eyes of Lori, the woman I couldn't seem to live without and who occupied all my dreams and thoughts. My heart was torn as I rolled the window down. I didn't want her to know how much I cared, how much I wanted her.

Hurt and worry were visible in her eyes.

"Is something wrong? What are you doing here?" She didn't try to hide her concern or her anger.

"No. Nothing's wrong."

Little Robbie barked his greeting.

"Hey, Robbie. Does your mistress have you out for a walk?"

The dog barked again, dancing around on his hind legs, his front paws waving in the air.

"No, we've already had our walk. We were across the street at the park."

"You aren't using your crutch. How come?"

"I don't need it any longer." She waved her hand in dismissal. "Enough idle chit-chat. Quit avoiding my question. Why are you here?"

I had to see you. My throat tightened painfully. I looked out the front window, then back at her.

"Want to go for a ride? I rarely get a chance to blow the cobwebs out of the engine on this jitney. I thought I'd do it today since I seem to have plenty of time on my hands and the doctor said I could drive now."

"Well, I don't have plenty of time. I have papers to grade and a work plan to revise. But thanks for stopping by." She stepped back, crossing her arms over her chest, staring at me, while Robbie sat looking from her to me and back again.

"I'll treat you to dinner. I know this little family restaurant a short distance out of town. You'll love their food." I could see she was about to say no again. "I hate eating alone. Please, come with me." I added a little whine to my voice.

She studied me like I was an wayward child.

"Please." I begged, desperately needing her to come with me. Crossing my heart, I said, "I promise to have you back early."

"Before I say yes, what is your real reason?"

"I missed you." There it was plain and simple.

She studied me for several uncomfortable seconds.

"All right. But I've got to be back early to grade papers."

"I'll even help you grade the papers, if you'd like."

"I need to put Robbie in the house and change clothes. Do you want to come up?"

"No, I'll wait here."

"Suit yourself."

She walked off and out of sight, while I drummed my fingers on the steering wheel.

I had missed Lori. In fact, I ached with longing. But I didn't want complications, didn't need them, yet, here I sat. I knew I couldn't leave if my life depended on my going.

Man, I had it bad.

Maybe if Lori and I dated a few times, I'd see we weren't compatible. Maybe then I would get her out of my system.

I scoffed at my gibberish thoughts.

My heart tightened at the sight of Lori as she walked out the gate and headed for my car. The woman was everything I wanted in a wife and more.

Drawn to her like a magnet, I wished we had stayed polar opposites—sniping and picking at one another—much safer that way. So much better for her. Much better for my peace of mind.

She slipped inside the car and the soft smell of flowers I associated only with Lori filled the Mustang. She reached around for the seatbelt and fastened it before looking at me.

In that moment, I wanted to take her in my arms and tell her how I felt about her. Instead, I turned on the ignition and backed out of the parking space.

"Well, are you going to tell me what this is all about?" She pointed at me, and then herself. "Or is this a game of a thousand questions until I land on the correct one?"

"What do you mean?" I headed toward the freeway.

"Okay." Releasing an exasperated breath, she shrugged. "I'll play along. But fair warning, I *will* have all my answers before this night is over."

She glanced around. "This is a great car. I bet it can get out and fly."

"It can. And if you promise not to tell the cops, every once in a while, I take her out into the country on a deserted road, and tromp the peddle, kicking all the soot out of her tailpipes while she purrs like a kitten."

"Your secrets safe with me,"—her face became one of a negotiator—"as long as you let me drive her. Otherwise, I have a detective friend ..."

"Wow, you sure know how to get your way."

She gave a confident shrug.

"How 'bout on our way back?" This was a first. I never allowed anyone to drive my Cobra. *Why Lori?*

"Really?" She looked wide-eyed.

"Really." I laughed, loving how she had already brightened my day just being in her presence.

"You're seriously going to trust me not to have a wreck in your precious car?"

135

"Are you that bad of a driver?"

"No, I've never had a wreck. Not even a fender-bender. But one never knows what will happen on down the road."

"I have faith in you."

"Thanks for your vote of confidence."

Her smile lit up her face and my world.

"How's your wound? Still sore?"

"A little. Still mending." *Don't ask her.* "What happened? After I was released from the hospital, I never saw you again."

"You've got to be kidding. You ask me what happened?"

"No, I'm not kidding." Although I had a pretty good idea.

"Well, let me see. The last time I visited, I had the distinct impression I was becoming a nuisance. So I figured I'd give you some space."

"I'm sorry if I left you with that impression. Chalk it up to the pain meds or not feeling well."

Chalk it up to fighting my attraction to you.

"I could have used your company these last few weeks." *More like I was a miserable, cranky man without you.*

"You could have fooled me." She crossed her arms compressing her lips.

She made me feel like one of her students in trouble.

"Do you have a cell phone?"

"What?" Her question threw me off kilter.

"A cellphone? Do you have one?"

"You know I do." I wasn't sure where she was going.

"Is it broken or lost?"

"No." Now I knew exactly where she was heading.

"Precisely." She tapped her chin with her finger. "*Hmm.* Isn't that odd?"

"What's odd?"

136

"My phone is working too. And my number hasn't changed. But I didn't receive a single call from you. Not even a voicemail, saying *hey, Lori, I'd sure love to see you. Would you come over for a visit, please?*"

"I'm sorry."

She shrugged. "After the way you ignored me in the hospital, I figured you needed your space. I also decided, you could call me when you were good'n ready to see me."

"Hey, listen, I was a jerk. I admit it. I'm sorry."

"You were a jerk, weren't you? Don't worry about it." She shrugged. "I was too busy to notice."

"Please, accept my apology for my terrible behavior. I'll do my best not to let that happen again."

"Acknowledged, and forgotten."

"Just like that?"

"Yes, just like that. Unless you'd like me to rake you over the coals, and then put you on a spit to roast."

Chuckling, I said, "No, ma'am. We're good then?" I gave her a quick glance, knowing she would answer when she was good and ready.

She nodded. "We're good."

We drove along in silence. The scenery along the road went from buildings to houses, to open land, taking us farther away from Dallas.

"Exactly where is this restaurant?" Her brows were knitted together, making two tiny fine lines in the middle.

"In Greenville."

"Greenville. I don't have time to go that far. I told you I had papers to grade and work to do."

I reached over, took hold of her hand, interlocking my fingers with hers. She didn't resist, which was a good sign.

"I'll turn around if you insist." I prayed she wouldn't. "I've been cooped up in my house for days. I was in need of something more than four walls. I figured a ride in the country would do the trick, especially now since I have you to enjoy, too." I smiled, hoping to break through her reserve.

Having Lori beside me was doing more to change my outlook than the ride itself, a little fact I wasn't about to tell her though.

One could say, I was playing with fire and they'd be right. But I couldn't resist.

Keeping my distance from Lori was like having Blue Bell ice cream in the freezer only a few feet away. Too enticing. Too impossible to ignore. Staying away from her was one of the most difficult things I had ever done in my life. Not until this moment, did I realize how important she was to me.

Rubbing my thumb over the back of her hand, I said, "I'm sorry. Will you forgive me?"

"I already said I would. End of discussion."

Seeing a pull out up ahead, I moved off the road into the small drive and parked.

"Lori, against my better judgment, I can't seem to stay away from you."

"Wow, do you expect me to say thanks?" Her brows rose.

"No, you misunderstood."

"Then enlighten me, please." She crossed her arms staring at me.

"I wasn't looking for love. In fact, I wanted nothing to do with it."

"*Hmm*, interesting."

It was all coming out wrong. I could tell she was getting ticked.

Normally, I was in control and could convey my thoughts in a clear, concise manner. With Lori, I felt like a tongue-tied teen, unable to get the right words to come out of my mouth.

"When I met you, all that changed. You consume my thoughts. I'm miserable without you." I ran a hand across my brow hoping I could make her comprehend how desperately I loved her.

"What you don't understand, I made plans for my life. Loving you has messed up all those plans. And though I've tried my best to be indifferent toward you, I can't. I don't want—"

The fury in her eyes stopped me.

"What? What did I say?"

"You've got to be kidding." Her laugh became filled with sarcasm. She clasped her hands tightly in her lap. "If you don't know, far be it for me to explain. I'd like to go home now."

"Please, Lori, tell me what I said to upset you?"

"Oh, nothing much, except I feel like I have been dropped into a bad remake of *Pride and Prejudice*. Your quasi-declaration is more like a B-rated reenactment of Darcy's declaration to Elizabeth. And personally, I don't like your confession of love any more than Elizabeth liked Darcy's."

The woman was talking nonsense. "I don't understand. Who is this Elizabeth and Darcy? What did I say to set you off?"

"Well, let me see if I can explain." She narrowed her eyes, her mouth in a straight line.

"To begin with, you don't want to love me, but you do, and against your better judgment, it would seem. If you thought your words would even begin to make me swoon at your feet, then you're wrong. I don't want any man who has to go against his own conscience to proclaim his undying love for me. Is that plain enough?"

"Yes, but you don't—"

"Take me home, please." She stared out the front window tapping her foot.

139

"Lori, please."

"Seth, take me home. I'd get out and walk if it weren't too far, but since it is ..." She gave an indifferent shrug.

I thought she was teasing. Her cold shoulder, crossed arms, and tapping foot had me scrambling to remember what I'd said and how the avowal of my love for her could go so wrong.

"Lori, I'm sorry if—" A tap on the window had me turning to look.

A uniformed police officer stood outside motioning for me to roll down my window, which I complied. All the while, I wished I had the power to send him into outer space.

Getting my irritation under control, I read his name off the badge "Hi, Officer Taylor. Is there something I can do for you?" I was plainly puzzled why he'd stopped behind me, flashing lights and all.

"Are you having car trouble, sir?"

"No sir, no car trouble." I smiled, mumbling, "More like girl trouble."

"Well, this isn't Lover's Lane. You can't park here." He bent down to look inside the car at Lori and then at me before standing again. "I need to see your license and proof of insurance."

"All right, just a moment." I pulled my driver's license and police identification from my wallet, handing them both to him before reaching for the glove compartment.

"Sorry, Detective Singleton."

"Seth."

"Seth." He smiled. "I won't need that." He handed me my I.D. "What are you doing in these parts?"

"Heading to Greenville for dinner." I looked over at Lori's rigid features and then shrugged. "But I think my companion has changed her mind. She wants to head back to Dallas."

Her undisguised snort of contempt came across loud and clear.

I didn't have a clue as to what had set her off. Maybe she expected flowers and down on one knee. *Women!* I was beginning to wonder why I was even trying to convince Lori that I loved her.

Officer Taylor stood back and gave the Mustang an appreciative look. "Sweet ride. Did you rebuild her yourself?"

"No. It belonged to my grandfather. He had it in a garage up under a car cover until it was passed down to me. Just had to do minor repairs—tune up, new carburetor, tires, things like that." I didn't want to pass the time of day with Officer Taylor. I needed to clear things with Lori.

Taylor whistled. "You don't find many old cars this clean. What is it, a '78, '79?"

"You were spot on the first time. It's a '78."

"She sure is a beauty." He slapped the top. "Well, I won't hold you any longer. Have a safe trip."

"Will do. If you're ever in Dallas, I hope you'll stop by the precinct and look me up."

"Thanks, I'll do that. Enjoy the ride." He tipped his hat before walking back to his squad car.

Once again, I glanced at Lori. "Are you sure you don't want to eat first?"

"I'm certain. Just take me home, Seth."

"All right." I studied her, wondering what was going on. "Would you like to drive? I *did* promise that you could drive on the way back."

"No. *Umm*, on second thought, yes, I would like to drive."

I wasn't sure what changed her mind, but if it was the car, I hoped it would put her in a more receptive frame of mind. Hopefully, she wouldn't try to blow the engine like her top had blown.

141

We got out to exchange places, crossing in front of the car. I didn't receive so much as a look from Lori. She got in behind the wheel, adjusted the seat and mirrors before taking off. And though it seemed strange sitting in the passenger seat, it gave me the perfect opportunity to study her.

Quiet and brooding, she looked straight ahead, ignoring me completely. Her little nose, slightly tilted upward, her luscious lips in a straight line, her stubborn chin held out. For some reason, I knew I was in deep trouble.

While living at home, my sisters would sometimes get peeved and then ignore me like Lori was doing now. With my sisters, I learned to ignore them and eventually they would come back around. But if not, it didn't bother me, but Lori *was* troubling me.

Ignoring Lori was a matter of a different sort, and a whole lot tougher to do. Though I didn't know what I had done or said, somehow I'd made a big blunder.

The best course of action, keep my mouth shut and ride out the storm. Hopefully, it would blow over before we got back to her apartment. Otherwise, no telling when, or if, I would get her to speak to me again. And she mattered *way* too much to allow a petty disagreement—whatever it was—to stand in the way of our happiness.

I mulled over her words about me being like Darcy, whoever the poor guy was. Still clueless to what she meant or what I'd said to tick her off in the first place, I figured it might be better not to know. Maybe let sleeping dogs lie, or in this case, give Lori time to simmer down. Eventually, she'd let me know what was eating at her. At least, I hope she would.

Chapter 16

Lori

"We've talked about my job, your class, your ankle, my wound, my sister, your brother, our parents even how much you like driving my car. Now that we have exhausted most of our topics and avoided the real issue, would you like to explain what you meant back there about that Darcy guy? I still don't understand what I said to tick you off."

I glanced over at him. "Do you actually want to start this on an empty stomach?" I didn't want to open up the subject at all. But it appeared Seth was determined to, regardless.

"If you remember, I tried to feed you in Greenville. I even suggested several places along the way, like Soulman's Barbeque in Royce City. But if I remember correctly, you said you weren't hungry."

"True. But now I'm starving. Where to?" I knew I was being difficult, but I couldn't help it. Seth needed to learn I had feelings. He also needed to learn he couldn't trample on them and expect me to roll over and play all gracious and happy.

"How does Gloria's sound?"

"Delicious. I love their black bean dip. I could make a meal out of their chips, salsa, and dip."

"Take the next exit then."

Seth gave me directions until we arrived at our destination.

The restaurant sat on a small rise overlooking Lake Ray Hubbard. What a shame it wasn't late spring. It would have been nice to sit out on the patio and eat, that is, if I were in a better mood. I still couldn't believe Seth's proposal, if that was what it was.

Seth requested a table by the windows. Since we had a little time to wait, I excused myself and made a quick trip to the ladies room.

While washing my hands, I looked into the mirror and did some soul searching. Something I didn't want to verbalize was staring me in the face. I loved Seth. The same man who could aggravate me at the snap of a tortilla chip.

I didn't want to admit he was the embodiment and more of what I looked for in a man. But did he love me? Or had he spoken earlier because he thought me indifferent and now I was a game he couldn't lose?

That was something I meant to find out.

The view out our window was spectacular. We gave the waiter our order then munched on chips and salsa infused dip.

"*Mmm*, this is so good." I bit into another chip.

"I can tell." He laughed and then turned serious. "What happened earlier? I honestly want to know so I can fix it. I can truthfully say I have no idea what took place, or what I said that came out so wrong."

"Can this wait until after we've eaten?"

"Sure."

He looked disappointed but didn't push for an answer.

The waiter brought our food, and though I was hungry and loved Gloria's Salvadorian/Tex-Mex, some of the pleasure had gone out of the meal. I needed to make sure

Seth wanted me for myself and not because I'd ignored him after he'd snubbed me.

"Why did you come to my apartment today?"

Seth put down his fork, studying me, no doubt weighing his words.

"To tell the truth, when I started out this afternoon, I had no intentions of going to your apartment. It just turned out I ended up there."

He was deep in thought as he fiddled with his iced-tea glass, rubbing his finger over the frost formed on the outside.

"I've missed you, Lori. For some inexplicable reason, I couldn't stay away. I had an overwhelming desire to see you, even if you didn't want to see me." He set his jaw, then relaxed. "Why did you stop coming to visit me after I got out of the hospital?"

"You've got to be kidding." I grunted. "Do you really need to ask?"

He shook his head, a pitiful grin place. "No. I'll admit it. I *was* pretty obnoxious. But I did that to protect you."

"By being rude and treating me like an unwanted guest, you were protecting me?"

He nodded.

"Wow. Do me a favor. Don't protect me anymore." I laughed. The guy wasn't making sense, but I had to ask. "Protecting me from what?"

"To keep me from falling in love with you. I didn't want you to love me."

"Well, thanks for doing me a big favor." I wiped my lips, wishing I could wipe the bitter taste from my mouth. "And you don't have to worry about me. It worked."

He gave me a questioning look.

I chuckled, feeling anything but happy. "I can say I'm fully Seth-proof now."

"No, you've got it all wrong." He reached for my hand.

I buried it in my lap, hiding the hurt his confession had brought.

"Wrong? I got it wrong?" I took a breath, trying my best to calm down.

"Let me see if I can summarize you correctly. You fought falling in love with me to spare my feelings, all the while fighting your attraction to me. You actually believed your rude behavior would help do the trick?" I laughed. "It worked. I'm completely turned off by you."

"Lori, please, you've misunderstood my meaning." The waiter came by. Seth motioned him away. "At the time, I was doing my best to protect you by making you dislike me." He waved his hand. "I know. It doesn't make any sense. Blame it on the drugs, if you want to. Whatever. I wasn't thinking straight."

This time, I studied him. "Seth, cut to the chase. What is it you want from me?"

"I want you." He pleaded with his eyes for understanding.

"And just what does *I want you* involve?"

"Everything." He rubbed the back of his neck, clearly agitated. "Let me start from the beginning."

I crossed my arms, willing to hear him out.

"At first, I enjoyed our sparring matches."

"I'm glad one of us did."

He chuckled. "I'm sorry. I know I was hard on you at times."

"Really? Let me count the ways." I held out my hands and began ticking off each digit. When I had no more to count, I said, "It looks like I've run out of fingers. Maybe I should take off my boots and start with my toes."

"No, please don't. We might get thrown out of the restaurant."

"Hum. You're probably right. I'll keep them on." I stared at him. "You were saying?"

"That's another thing I love about you, your zany sense of humor."

I wouldn't tell Seth that his compliment had me glowing inside. Let him squirm. See if he could extricate himself from the hole he'd dug and was now standing in ... or should I say, sitting in?

He shook his head. "Where was I?"

"I believe you were about to tell me how you tormented me to keep me at a distance."

"I didn't torment you."

"Then what would you call it? Tease, taunt, bait, goad, needled? Mere semantics. I believe you will find all of these words and more are the definition of torment."

"You've got me there."

"Yes, I believe I do, and I'm loving it."

"I know better than to argue with a school teacher."

"Smart man." I smiled, raising my brows. "Continue."

"Picking on you, even sparring with you was my way of keeping you close but at a distance. You see, from the beginning there was something that drew me to you. And now there's nothing about you that I don't love. I love your laugh, your compassion, even how you can take my sarcasm, turn it around, and use it against me."

He glanced down at the tablecloth, running his finger over a crease, before looking up at me. "Lori, what I'm trying to say is I care deeply about you. I didn't want to, but I do. Even now, somehow against my better judgment, I can't seem to help myself."

"Oh, wow! You sure know how to sweet-talk a girl. You love me against your better judgment. I wonder how I'd feel if you came right out and said you loved me, but you wished you didn't?" I gave a humorless chuckle. "I believe I'd be in ecstasy."

"I'm messing it up again. I'm trying to tell you how I feel. But I've had little practice, no, scratch that, I've had

147

no practice at all." He shrugged, wearing a silly grin. "If you can wait for five years, I'd like to marry you."

"Five years?" He wanted me to wait without a reason, without considering five years might be too long. And without coming straight out and saying the words *I love you*. How hard is that?

"Yeah. That gives me enough time to get my head around a desk job, and this marriage thing. We need to make sure this is what we both want."

"I'd like to go home now, please."

"Home?"

"Yes, home."

"Is that your answer?"

"It is for now. I want to go home."

"Is that a *no,* then?" Seth signaled for the check.

"If you think I am about to accept your proposal with little or no consideration of my feelings, then you're wrong. Five years is a long time to wait. Even for you." I wanted to add *and without so much as an I love you.*

We were both silent as we walked out of the restaurant.

Instead of asking if I wanted to drive, he opened the passenger door and waited for me to get in, and then with a heavy hand, slammed the door. I could tell as he walked around the front of the car he wasn't in good spirits.

Well, neither was I.

When he got behind the driver's seat, he didn't take so much as a look in my direction once.

I mulled over his words and knew I was correct. Seth never once came right out and said I love you. He weaseled every which way but didn't come up to bat. In fact, he'd quite adamantly objected to loving me, if love was what he actually felt.

Still, I wasn't sure how I felt about him either. I thought I loved him. I was miserable without him. I even enjoyed his company, *at times*. Definitely, anytime I was around him, my emotions were tangled up in knots—unsure whether to dislike him and wanting him so bad it hurt.

How could I be so mixed up and confused? If only he'd said he loved me and then gave me a reason for the prolonged delay, I would have waited the five years easily. *Or would I?*

Seth was well worth the wait, but ... why wait that long if you truly loved someone?

Chapter 17

Seth

Women! Well, not all women, but definitely one in particular ... *Lori.* I will never understand her as long as I live. Yet, I love her beyond reason. Since she didn't say *yes*, and she didn't say *no*, where did that leave us?

Maybe, I'll let her be for a while, and then she might come to a decision.

Come to think of it, the last time I left her alone got me in a truckload of trouble. It would be better to resolve this now than to ignore it altogether. Maybe if I showed her how much I want to be around her, then she'll know how much I love her.

Knowing she should be out of school by now, I dialed her number but got her voicemail. Not wanting to leave a message, I disconnected. What I had to say to her couldn't be said over the phone.

Needing to clear my head and maybe get a better perspective what to do next, I decided to go for a ride. Before I knew it, my Jeep and I were parked in front of Lori's apartment again.

When I got out of my vehicle, I heard Robbie barking, and then saw her and the dog across the street at that quasi-park/vacant lot. Instead of crossing the street and joining her, I leaned my hip against the backend, crossing my legs and my arms as I watched.

She threw a ball, and Robbie bounded after it. When he brought it back to her, she rubbed and patted his head and then threw it again.

To say she was beautiful with the sun chasing gold through her hair was an understatement.

She raised her hand to brush back the few strands the wind had blown across her cheeks. I wanted to be that wind, touching her hair.

Man, I had it bad. I was practically drooling over the woman while, as the poets would say, waxing eloquently of her loveliness. *Get a grip.*

Robbie, romped through the grass, retrieved the ball, and then trotted back to Lori's side. He dropped the ball and barked.

Lori squatted and ruffled the dog's head, then threw the ball again. Like an arrow released from a bow, Robbie's small black body shot out across the field after the ball, while Lori yelled encouragements to the dog.

Unable to resist any longer, I strolled across the street to join her, hoping she wouldn't object. I had barely reached the curb when I saw Gregg leaning against the tree much like I had leaned against my Jeep seconds earlier. He shoved away from the trunk and sauntered over to where Lori stood.

They began talking.

He laughed aloud.

Lori looked at Gregg and smiled.

Violent tendencies were foreign to me. However, I wanted to punch the guy's lights out and then plow him underground before shoveling dirt over him. He had no business being here with Lori, not when I loved her and had made it clear I wanted us to get married.

Had she invited Gregg? Just thinking about it, made my blood boil.

Here I stood, too quick to judge when I didn't know all the facts? I dealt with facts every day. Proved innocence or guilt of a person by facts. But now I was ready to believe the worst of the woman I loved.

What had gotten into me? *Jealousy*, of course.

I knew the moment Lori saw me. She smiled and waved, a question in her gaze.

Gregg looked in my direction but didn't appear any too happy to see me.

Whatever happened to that background check on Gregg?

Oh, yeah. I was shot, is what.

First thing, I'll call Tim and see what, if anything, he has found on the guy.

Robbie barked and came running at me. I squatted and held out my arms catching the dog in midair. He tried to lick me while squirming in my arms, something Lori previously warned me Robbie wasn't supposed to do. So I snuggled him in the crook of my arm and gave him a good rubdown. I ran my hand over his head and down his back several times, talking to him, before releasing him to run back to Lori.

I followed the dog.

Lori, her hand shielding her eyes against the sun, watched me until I came up to her.

Unable to tell whether she was happy to see me or not, I smiled. "Hey, beautiful, how are you doing?" I would have kissed her but felt that was pressing my luck.

"Fine. I didn't think you'd drop by today." She gave me a puzzled look.

"I didn't either. But I had an insatiable desire to see you." I smiled, knowing I was laying my heart open for Lori to slice and dice if she wanted to. If I were going to marry her, I would have to trust her with not just my heart, but with my soul, and so much more. "So here I am."

"So I see."

I bent and kissed her on the cheek, hoping she wouldn't slap me. The light kiss astounded her as much as it did me. "By the way, you look gorgeous today."

She smiled, acting a little off kilter. "Thanks."

I meant the compliment and wanted to say so much more but held back because of our audience.

Turning to Gregg, I said. "Hi, how are you doing?"

I held out my hand, when what I would have rather done was flattened his nose against his face for being here with Lori.

Man! Where this guy was concerned I was having some major anger issues. I was going to have to work on my attitude.

"I'm fine. Lori told me about you being shot. I hope you're healing up well." He glanced at Lori and me, looking confused.

Play it cool. Instead of telling him to back off, I said, "I am, thanks."

"Robbie." Lori clapped her hands, pulled the leash from her pocket. "Come here, boy." She knelt on the grass waiting for the dog to come to her.

The dog ran to me instead.

"Traitor." Smiling, she held out the leash. "Here, since it appears he wants you to walk him, you can do the honors."

I hooked the leash to Robbie's collar. He started dancing around, eager to get started. "Where to?"

She turned to Gregg. "We're going for a walk, so I'll see you later. Have a good evening."

"You too."

Lori motioned to the sidewalk. "If you're up to it, we'll walk him around the block."

153

"I'm up to it, as long as you're by my side." I held out my hand willing her to take hold.

When she hesitated, I said, "Unless that's asking too much."

She slipped her fingers in mine, her touch making everything right with the world. Maybe she wasn't as upset with me as I thought she would be. When I turned to look at Gregg, he was watching us. He smiled and waved, then started off across the street to the apartments.

I still didn't like that guy. There was something about him that grated against my nerves, and it had nothing to do with Lori.

"Does this mean I can count on seeing you on a regular basis in the afternoon to help me walk Robbie?"

My thoughts turned from Gregg to Lori. "Would you want me to?" My heart stopped, hoping she would say *yes*, but afraid she'd say *no*.

"Yes." She glanced down at her feet. A smile tugged at the corner of her mouth.

"Then I'll be here, at least until I go back to work, which will be another week and a half." Not wanting to press my luck, yet, unable to stop myself I said, "I could take you to work and pick you up until I go back."

Teetering on the edge, I expected her to shoot down my offer.

"Hmm, I'll have to give that some thought.

Ecstatic she hadn't turned me down outright, I said "And if you'd like, Robbie could spend his days at my house. What do you think?"

I held my breath hoping she'd agree, knowing if she did, she was practically making a commitment.

She chewed on her bottom lip, then raised her brows. "Robbie would like that. But I think he might be too much for you?"

Wanting to punch the air in victory, I smiled instead. "He wouldn't be any trouble." I held the leash to the side. "You've seen how he and I get along. And I've got a huge back yard with a wildlife park backing up to my property." I watched her. "So what about you? Would you like a ride to work for the next week and a half?"

Seeing her cute little grin, I knew she was up to something. Thankfully, she wasn't still upset with me.

"*Hmm*. It would save me money on gas. And I wouldn't have to drive in the traffic."

"Well, I'm all for saving you money and the frustration of traffic."

She tapped her chin, a devilish glint in her eye, and then dragged her lower lip between her teeth. "If I say yes, do you think we could have a police escort if I wake up late any of those days?"

"You're impossible." I picked her up and twirled her around, while Robbie danced around my feet. "But I love you just the same. And no, a police escort is not doable."

At first, she looked as if she'd been hit by a stun gun, before giving me a huge smile.

"Ahh, shucks." She shrugged. "But I'll still take you up on your offer."

"Good."

"That is, if you meant what you said."

Now I was the one confused. "Meant what?"

"You've got to be kidding." She puckered her brow. "How easily words tumble from your mouth."

It dawned on me what she referred to. I stopped walking and turned to her, putting both my arms around her waist. "I didn't forget. And it wasn't said in jest. I love you, Lori."

I dipped my head and planted a kiss on her lips … lips that melted under my touch while I showed her just how much I loved her.

Decency won out. I didn't want to embarrass Lori with a public display of my affection. Not that I didn't want the world to know how much I loved her, I did.

When I pulled back, I said. "It may have taken me a little while to realize the truth. But when I found you too hard to resist, I knew what I felt wasn't mere attraction.

"I love you, Lori, and always will."

"Oh, Seth." She grabbed me by the neck. "That's what I've been waiting to hear you say. And you know what?"

"No, what?"

"I love you back." Pulling my head down, she gave me a gentle kiss that went all through me, affecting me more than the kiss we shared seconds ago.

Robbie started barking, prancing around.

"I think the little fellow wants to finish his walk."

"Yep, I think you're right." Lori hooked her arm through mine. "Seth, are you sure?"

"I wouldn't have said the words unless I meant them. I love you, Lori. So much so, I can't imagine life without you."

"*Hmm*. Then why do you want to wait five years to get married?"

Not wanting to anger her by saying something stupid, I took a moment to prepare my answer.

"When I said I would like to wait five years to get married, I was thinking of you."

"Me?"

"Yeah. Being a detective comes with hazards."

She wrinkled her nose. "I don't live in a bubble, Seth. I know there are hazards with your job. I'm willing to accept them. But why wait? What you do won't change five years from now."

We turned the corner, and Robbie knew we were on the home stretch. He began pulling on his leash.

"Don't let him pull. He knows better. Make him heel." She frowned. "If you're going to take care of him for a week or so, you can't undo what I've worked hard to make him learn."

"Yes, ma'am." Smiling, I gave a slight jerk on the leash. "Heel."

Robbie stopped, cocked his head at me curiously, then began walking alongside my leg.

"Good boy." I looked at her.

"Back to my job. In about five years I'll be more resolved to take a desk job, where I process papers instead of going after criminals. That way, you won't have to worry if I'll come home at night or end up in the hospital or worse."

We reached the entrance to her apartment.

She punched my arm.

"What was that for?" I rubbed the spot pretending her little punch hurt.

"For trying to persuade me to your side. But we'll have the remainder of this conversation inside."

I opened the gate. She and Robbie passed through. "Lori, you don't understand."

"I do. But like I said, we'll finish our discussion inside."

"I can just bet your students are deathly afraid of crossing you."

She stiffened her back, frowning. "Why do you say that? My kids love me."

"Oh, I know they do. They can't help but. However, I don't believe you tolerate any nonsense with them either."

"If by that you mean I'm in full control at all times, then yes, that's true. I don't tolerate any nonsense in my class, and they know it. Otherwise, my students wouldn't learn a thing."

I nodded, knowing I didn't stand a chance. When Lori got something in her head, she probably wouldn't let it go until she had all the answers, and they were all to her satisfaction.

We reached the apartment, and she unlocked the door. Inside the entry, she unsnapped the leash, and Robbie took off for his water bowl.

"I was going to order pizza for dinner. Would you like to stay and eat with me?" She looked a little uncertain.

"Yeah, if I can make two requests."

"And they are?"

"I pay, and at least half of the pizza is fully loaded."

"No, I asked you, so it's my treat."

"Then that's a deal breaker." I shrugged, trying to look unconcerned.

"What if I say I will order the whole pizza fully loaded, will you change your mind?" She smiled trying her best to convince me to her way of thinking.

"Nope, I'm sorry. It's all or none. A fully loaded pizza and I pay."

Frowning, she crossed her arms. "Has anyone ever told you, you can be one very stubborn man?"

I shook my head. "No, not until just now."

"You lie."

Smiling, I pulled her into the circle of my arms. "Maybe a little. But you might as well give up, because I'm going to win this one." I kissed the tip of her nose.

"However, I propose a compromise."

She hooked her arms around my neck. "What is your compromise?"

"Do you have salad fixings?"

"Yes."

"Then you can supply the salad and drinks, I'll supply the pizza and the pleasure of my company. Deal?"

"Your compromise is what others would call a bribe. I figured you, Detective Singleton, were above bribery."

Leaning in, I gave her a quick kiss on the lips. "I will try bribery, even coercion, if it means I get my way where you're concerned, Ms. Morgan." This time, I kissed her soundly on the mouth, spinning my emotions into overdrive.

Still reeling from our kiss, I released her and dug into my pocket for my cell phone. I punched the number of a pizza joint not too far from Lori's, knowing full well if I didn't, my moratorium of a five-year waiting period would be history. Lori and I would be standing before Pastor Steve saying I do in a matter of months instead.

And for certain, though I loved her with all my heart, soul, and being, I wasn't about to let that happen.

Chapter 18

Lori

"Hang up."

Seth looked at me as if I were crazy. "Hang up?"

"Yes. We can order pizza later. Right now, I have questions that need to be answered."

He pocketed his cell phone, a little weary looking.

"What just happened?"

"I'm not sure I know what you mean?" Seth looked around my living room but not at me.

"You kissed me like there was no tomorrow, and just like that"—I snapped my fingers—"you're calling for pizza. I don't think so."

He stood before me like a repentant child, a silly grin lurking on his lips.

Wanting to stomp my foot, I refrained. He apparently didn't understand just how put out I was with him.

"You're either starving to death, or my kiss didn't meet your standard requirements. So, which was it?" I pounced my hands on my hips.

"My what?" Seth reached for me. "Come here."

Shaking my head, I moved back out of reach.

"You're not getting off that easily, Buster. What's going on?"

Though he tried his best to conceal his thoughts, I could see a war was going on in his mind.

"*Ah*, Princess ..."

"Don't *ah Princess* me. That will get you exactly nowhere. And, I'm not your princess ... *yet*."

I didn't want to feel anything, but he was a master at worming his way into my heart. His tender voice, along with the love shining from his eyes, softened me. However, I wasn't going to give in to him, at least not yet.

"Lori, you're my princess, my love, and so much more." He held out his arms again. "Come here, *please?*"

I didn't want to comply, but my heart and legs decided for me.

He smelled so good and felt even better when I slipped into his arms and nestled up against him. *Natural* was the word that came to mind. This was where I belonged.

Resting my cheek against his chest, I listened to the steady beat of his heart as if our hearts beat as one.

"I don't have standard requirements, Princess. But if I did, your kiss would have far exceeded anything I could have hoped or dreamed. The way you fit in my arms, even the way you smell, drives me crazy to where I can't think straight. If we go on like now"—he shrugged—"my five-year plan is as good as gone."

He breathed in deeply. "By that I mean, I won't be able to resist marrying you. My plan is, in five years I'll take a desk job. That way, what happened to my Aunt Rachel won't happen to you."

Pulling back, staying in the circle of his arms, I saw he was serious.

"What happened to your aunt that you're afraid will happen to me?"

Seth released me, took hold of my hand and led me to the sofa.

"Sit down. I'll explain."

"Please do and don't you dare leave anything out." After sitting and pulling my legs beneath me, I waited for him to begin.

Seth shoved one of the armchairs up close, facing me, and then took my hand in his.

"Lori, I told you playing cops and robbers was one of the reasons I became a cop, which is partially true. However, the other reason was my Uncle Dale. He was a police detective, who I admired greatly.

"One day, my Aunt Rachel received a call every policeman hopes will never be made. After thirty-five years on the job and three months short of retirement, my uncle was shot and killed by a drug kingpin."

I squeezed his hand, wanting him to know his sorrow was mine. "Ah, Seth, I'm so sorry."

"Thanks, love." He stared at my hand as if it was the most important thing in the world. "However, the purpose of telling you is so you will understand my reasoning to wait."

His face revealed pain as he bowed his head, no doubt reliving the awful memories.

"Standing over my uncle's grave, I made a promise to myself to catch his killer, which has proven difficult. We know the name of his operation, 'The Company,' but not who he is or what he looks like."

Though I understood his logic to find his uncle's killer, I wasn't sure I agreed. I knew he'd be in constant danger if he continued to pursue the drug lord, which, added to my fear … Seth could end up like his uncle.

"My Aunt Rachel was all upset that I had made such a promise. I told her I'd give it another five years in which to find and bring the criminal to justice. If I didn't succeed by then, I'd put it to bed and walk away."

He glanced up at me. "That's why I need us to wait to get married for at least five years. If I get close to the man, you, and anyone else who is dear to me, stands the chance of being in jeopardy, especially if we're married or have children. He would use you as leverage."

"Surprisingly, I understand you're flawed reasoning, even if I don't agree with it." I shrugged. "By the sheer nature of your job, you're in danger every day. So I don't see how today or five years on down the road will make a great deal of difference as far as we are concerned."

Releasing my hand, he folded his together, leaning his elbows on his knees. "I appreciate you being candid with me."

Seeing his downcast appearance, I knew he'd come to the wrong conclusion. "Seth ... you misunderstood what I was saying."

"To me it was clear. Instead of waiting five years, you'd rather not wait at all."

"Wow! You're living proof, men's minds do operate differently than women."

I shook my head. "In some respects what you say is true. However, I meant by *five years won't make a difference* is, you'll still be doing the same job, and it won't make a difference to me. So whether we get married five years from now or tomorrow won't change a thing. I'm willing to marry you regardless of the hazards of being a police detective's wife."

"What if I were to get shot again, or worse, killed?"

"What if you don't?" I raised my brows.

"Lori, you don't understand. I don't want you to live your days and nights wondering when or if I'll come back home to you alive and well. And my schedule is such that I sometimes pull down an all-nighter, or work 12-hour shifts.

"It's nothing for me to work 10-15 days without a day off. It's tough on a detective's wife and family, that is if we're blessed to have children."

163

Excitement filled me with thoughts of the intimacy of a husband and wife, and making babies with Seth, while heat rushed up my neck. Though it was something I looked forward to, I was too modest not to blush.

Clearing my throat, I said. "Let me put it this way, I knew what you did for a living when I met you. My brother told me.

"I won't lie and say it's what I had envisioned for my future husband. But it's what you do, and you do it well. Even the fact you are actively pursuing this drug lord, or that he could be a threat to me, doesn't change my mind in the least."

He frowned. "I don't want you to be, God forbid, threatened by someone I might be actively pursuing."

"Look at me." I lifted his head and turned his face toward me. "I want you to know what I say is true and that I mean it from my heart."

When I had his full attention, I continued. "I'm not the type to fret over *what ifs* or *maybes*. As far as you getting shot, you could be a doctor or lawyer, and still be killed on your way home, or keel over with a heart attack. Worse things have been known to happen."

"Lori, you say that now, but—"

Putting my finger to his lips, I said, "*Shh.* You've had your say. Now let me have mine."

"When haven't you?" He raised his brows, chuckling.

"Don't be snarky. And don't try to sidetrack me. It won't work." I gave him a stern stare, but I was hard put to keep my smile from showing.

"I know you are in active pursuit of this man, which, I won't lie, frightens me. But it doesn't make me want to walk away or wait till you decide, if ever, to take a desk job. Knowing this, I'll say an extra prayer or two or three or more for your safety." I smiled, before continuing. "Still, it won't stop me from loving you or wanting to be your wife."

Pausing to allow my words to sink in, yet not long enough so he'd butt in, I said, "You might as well accept it."

He looked at me quizzically.

"I'm not going away. And ... I'm not going to wait five years. So think on that Seth Singleton, and then you decide."

I knew I was putting my future, *no*, our future on the line.

"Do you love me enough to look past *your* fear? Or do you want to wait and miss out on five years of ecstatic love and happiness? Because that's what I see in our future if you'll stop being so stubborn."

While Seth sat there looking down at his hands, my stomach got tangled in knots. I wanted him, but did he want me enough to throw away his five-year plan to start our future now instead of waiting? Or was he going to let fear rule the day?

He looked up at me with determination in his eyes. Standing, he pulled me to my feet.

"Against my better judgment, Lori, if you will have me, I will marry you whenever and wherever you say." He hugged me up close then pulled back.

"Lori Morgan, will you do me the honor of becoming my wife?"

"For goodness sake, I thought you were never going to ask." Feeling emboldened, I tipped up, pulled his head toward mine, and kissed him soundly on the lips, and then leaned back, my senses reeling.

"My answer is ... yes, a thousand times, yes." Smiling I added, "And you will never regret this day. I mean to make you the happiest man on earth. Just you wait and see."

Chapter 19

Seth

What have I done?

Oblivious to the computer screen in front of me, questions and consequences swirled around in my head. This morning, in the light of day, I sat here second-guessing my decision to ask Lori to be my wife.

My love for Lori hadn't changed, nor did I doubt she loved me. What *had* changed, the reality that our wedding would take place in June, less than four months away.

We figured June would be perfect since Lori would be out of school and we could take a nice, long honeymoon. And after we returned, she would have the summer to get her things moved and arranged in our house. Hopefully, she'd also be accustomed to life as a detective's wife long before starting school again in August.

Being married to a cop would be a big adjustment—*my take on the situation, not hers.*

Love wasn't the challenge. Being married to me would be the real test. My schedule, the daily grind of coming home unable to talk about my cases, doing my best to clear my mind of the filth on the streets, and always wearing a gun. That's what Lori would have to live with married to me.

But could she? Was she strong enough?

I knew if she walked away from me today, it would be like ripping my heart from my chest. I would be a broken man—I loved her that much.

However, the inability to keep her safe 24/7 sat as the real crux of my problem and weighed heavy on my mind. How was I to know when you love someone this deeply, your ability to keep her safe and happy would weigh you down.

Robbie jumped up on my lap wanting my attention.

"Hey, little fellow, you know your mistress would have both our heads for you jumping up here uninvited."

The dog cocked his head to one side, then barked.

"I won't tell, but you will have to ask next time, understand?"

He barked again then laid his head down on my lap.

I ran my fingers through his soft hair, dozing off. Startled by my cellphone ringing, I grabbed it up.

"Hey, Tim. What's up?"

"Nothing much. Just thought I'd check on you. How are you feeling?"

"I'm great, just bored out of my skull. Robbie's company only goes so far, especially since his only means of communication is barking." I chuckled.

"You taking care of Lori's dog now? Is there something you'd like to tell me?"

Knowing Tim wouldn't let it drop till he'd ferreted out the whole truth, I figured I'd give him the lowdown.

"We're getting married in June."

"*Whoa-ho!* You sure don't do things by half measures." He laughed. "Congratulations. I always thought you and Lori were meant for each other." He paused. "I am going to be best man, aren't I?"

"Yes. But put a lid on it. I don't want it getting out until Lori is ready to tell her folks and mine."

"*Mums* the word. Wow! I still can't believe the great Seth Singleton is—"

"*Tim.*"

"Okay, okay. I'll change the subject, but I still can't believe it."

I grunted.

"Oh, yeah, my other reason for the call."

I didn't say anything, waiting on him to tell me the reason for the call.

"That morning you were shot you asked me to do some checking on Lori's neighbor, Gregg Lambert?"

"Yeah. I forgot about that. Did you find something?" Just thinking about Lambert caused no small amount of unrest.

"Sure did. Lambert is too squeaky-clean, if you ask me. Looking at his history, the guy must have taken a vow to become the cleanest guy on the universe or turned monk." Tim laughed.

"He's not a monk." I spit out. "Is there more?"

"There's no prior credit history, or credit cards, for that matter. His bank account is minimal. And another thing, when I checked with his neighbors at his prior address, no one seemed to have ever heard of a Gregg Lambert. Either his neighbors have short-term memory, or he was born the day he moved into Lori's apartment complex."

Tim made a scoffing noise. "If you ask me, this guy is begging us to dig deeper to find out who he actually is."

My criminal radar buzzed off the chart.

Robbie, who had been quiet while Tim was talking, must have felt my agitation. He whined, jumped down, and then ran over to his crate. The dog curled up in his bed, his big old black eyes watching me.

"I think you're right. Email me all the info you've found so far and I'll keep on searching from here."

I wanted nothing more than to go over there and haul Lambert's sorry backside in for questioning ... but for what? I'd be breaking all the laws I swore to uphold, not to mention his legal rights, if I did something so foolish.

"Will do. But listen, don't go all Rambo on me and try to take this guy on by yourself. I'm still your backup, even if you are out of commission for a few weeks. And you best keep this from Lori so she won't tip our hand."

"She wouldn't. But I don't intend on telling her unless we find he has a violent past, and then I'll bodily move her out of that apartment, if I have to."

"Man, I never thought I'd see the day Seth Singleton would be caught and hogtied so fast by a woman."

"I'm hanging up now."

"*Ooo-eee.* You've sure got it bad."

I disconnected with Tim laughing in my ear.

He was right. I had it worse than I ever thought possible, but I loved Lori to distraction. And now, she could have a serial killer or, God only knew, something worse practically living next door to her.

My gut was burning like gasoline had been poured down my throat and ignited. Her safety sat squarely on my shoulders, yet I felt like a helpless infant.

A ding alerted me I had email. I jiggled the mouse, making my screen active. By the time I read Tim's report, every fiber of my being was alert and itching to get this guy as far away as possible from Lori. I was ready to move her out tonight, but I knew I was acting unreasonable.

Furthermore, Lori would undoubtedly have none of it, which I could hardly blame her. I needed evidence this guy was a fugitive, not just my gut telling me he was one.

After making a few phone calls to fellow officer friends, who were more than willing to look deeper into

169

Lambert's background, I felt a little more in control. Still, common sense told me a man without a past couldn't be a good thing. He was hiding from someone. And I was going to find out who.

"Come on Robbie, it's time to pick up your mistress."

The dog's ears perked up, and he trotted out of his crate. This morning, I had swung by a pet store, bought a new crate, bed-pad, and all the paraphernalia that Robbie would need so I wouldn't be lugging everything back and forth from Lori's apartment to my house.

A plan formulated in my head, but I wasn't sure I could get Lori to go along with what I had in mind. If she didn't agree, then I'd be sleeping in front of her door.

After strapping Robbie in the backseat, I headed to Wilder Elementary to pick up Lori. The whole way there, I worked and reworked the details of the plan in my head, knowing it had to be just right or she would rebel.

Lori spotted me when I pulled up. She came out all smiles. I wonder how long her smile would last if I went about my plan the wrong way.

I hopped out and opened the door but stopped her before she could climb up into my Jeep.

"Hi, Princess." I pulled her into my arms and kissed her right there before God and everyone, not caring who saw us. When I released her, her cheeks were flushed, but other than that, she didn't object, and best of all, she was all smiles.

"Hi, yourself, handsome." She gave me a quick peck on the lips, then scrambled up into the car. "Hey, Robbie boy. I see you came to pick me up too." She turned around, got on her knees, and reached to give the dog a pat and a scratch under the chin before sitting down and buckling up.

"If this is what I can expect every day for the next week and a half, then I say *yes!*" She shot her fist into the air and then winked at me.

170

"However, my principal just might have something else to say about our public display of affection in front of the parents and students."

"Okay, this is what I'll do. When I pick you up tomorrow, we'll go around the block, stop, and do some kissing and necking there. How about that" I waited for her response.

"*Well*, I'm afraid that could get us into trouble, too."

"How so?"

"One thing could lead to another and before you know it, I'd have to call a good friend of mine who happens to be on the police force to bail us out."

"His name wouldn't happen to be Tim, would it?"

She snapped her fingers. "Yes, that's the fellow. I don't believe he'd be too happy bailing us out for necking in a residential neighborhood and shocking all the respectable homeowners. So how about a sweet, quick kiss, and leave the necking for later."

"Spoil sport. But you have a point. I know this Tim fellow. He just might leave us there to rot. So, as much as it will kill me to do so, I'll refrain."

"I knew I was marrying a smart guy."

Figuring there would be no better time than the present to lay the groundwork for my plan, I said, "Lori, I'd like to suggest something, but hear me out before you say no."

"Don't I always?"

I scoffed, "*Yeah, sure you do.* But seriously, I'd like you to move into my house—"

"What? Are you out of your mind?"

"I don't mean for us to move in together. That'll only happen after we're married."

"Thankfully. I was beginning to wonder."

"Hear me out before you say no."

"Okay, *and ...*"

171

"I propose that you move into my house. I will move into your apartment. That way, while I'm off, I can get some of my buddies to help move your furniture, except for the bed. I'll need that to sleep in until we're married."

"And I'm doing this why?"

"This way, over time, you'll have everything set up at the house as you want it, instead of having to rush around putting the house in order and preparing the wedding at the same time." I glanced over at her. "And you'll have more living space, a big back yard for Robbie, and a garage to park your car. What do you think?"

She gave me an incredulous look. "You're nuts, is what."

"No, I'm serious, Lori. Think about it. We can take anything you don't want of mine, store it in the garage, and then one weekend have a giant yard sale. That way we can get rid of what we don't want or need. And you'll have money in your pocket to buy whatever, or to use on the wedding."

"Seth, I can't move, set up our house, plan for our wedding, and keep up with my lesson plans. It would be a nightmare. No, we'll stick to the original plan. I'll move in once we're married."

She looked around at our surroundings. "Where are we going?"

"I thought you might want to see your future home. Who knows, the house might be a deal breaker."

"Don't even joke that way. It's not funny." She folded her arms and gave a disgusted grunt.

"Sorry." I turned onto my street and stopped the Jeep facing the house. I wanted Lori to get the full effect, hoping she'd like it.

"That's it." I motioned straight ahead.

"Oh, Seth. I wasn't expecting anything this nice. Your house is beautiful."

"Our house." I couldn't contain my pride. "I'm pleased you like it. Hopefully, you'll like the inside as well. I've updated the kitchen and bathrooms, but I'm willing to change anything you don't like. And paint is always cheap."

She touched my arm. Her sweet smile had me wanting to hold her and not let go.

"You want to look inside? I have a couple of steaks I can throw on the barbecue before taking you home."

"Sure, I'd love to see the house. And the steaks, *hmm* ..." She pursed her lips, then grinned. "Sounds good to me. Park this thing and let's go in."

Instead of pulling into the garage, I stopped on the drive. I ran around to open the door and help Lori down. Seeing my neighbor waving at us, I waved back.

"Hey, Seth."

"Hi, Ken." Since he was heading in my direction, I waited for him, thinking to introduce Lori.

"I thought you'd want to know, there was a man here asking about you."

"Did he leave a name?" I didn't like someone snooping around my house. I smiled though, not wanting to alarm Ken or Lori.

No one would casually drive through my neighborhood, and then stop to ask questions about me. It had to be someone who was up to no good.

"Dick Smith is the name he gave. He wanted to know what time you'd be home."

"He did, did he?" This guy, whoever he might be, was getting more disturbing by the second.

"Yeah. I told him you didn't keep regular hours. No need to give the man fair warning of your comings and goings, if you know what I mean."

"I do, and thank you, Ken." I looked at Lori's perplexed face. "Forgive my manners. Ken Cafferty, this is Lori

173

Morgan, my fiancée. Lori, this gentleman is my next-door neighbor, who is also a retired mail carrier of forty years." I smiled.

"Nice to meet you, Lori. And congratulations. My Mary will be quite pleased to learn Seth is getting married."

"Thank you." Lori shook Ken's hand. "It won't be until June, but with all I have to do, it will be here before I know it."

Ken nodded. "Well, sometime you're here, come on over and meet Mary. And if you ever need anything, just knock on the door. We'll be glad to help."

"I appreciate you letting me know about Dick Smith." I wanted Ken to understand I was grateful for his diligence as a neighbor.

"Well, when you're my age and have nothing better to do than be the neighborhood watch, having visitors out of the ordinary, brings a little excitement to my day." He laughed. "I'll see you later."

I retrieved Robbie from the backseat, then allowed him to be curious around the yard and do his business.

"That was strange. Do you know Dick Smith?"

Robbie joined us. I unlocked the door. "Can't say that I do."

She tilted her head, staring at me. "Why would a man you don't know come to your house and ask about you?"

"Beats me." I shrugged while motioning for her to enter. "Shall we, or do you want to stand out here and freeze."

"I'd rather be warm. But I still would like answers."

We walked into the entry. "I'm not likely to provide them because I don't know the man."

"Then why did he drop by? How did he know where your house was?"

I took her coat and hung it in the coat closet before doing the same with mine. "You sure are full of question I

174

can't answer. And if I didn't know better, I'd think you were the detective, not me."

She laughed.

Robbie ran straight into the washroom where his crate and bowls were stored.

"Come here, you." I reached out and grabbed her arm, swinging her around to face me. "I've wanted to do this ever since you gave me that little peck out in front of your school." I leaned down and captured her lips, savoring the taste of her, knowing how right she felt in my arms.

Lifting my head, I stared into her eyes that were filled with love. I knew if I didn't break this off now, I would be past the point of no return and unable to quit.

Grabbing her hand, I lead her into the living room, watching closely to see her reaction.

She looked pleasantly surprised. "I love the room. And I love how the open concept makes the living space appear even bigger. Usually, these old homes aren't this open. Yours is wonderful."

"It wasn't like this. I tore out the wall between the living and dining rooms, and opened the wall into the kitchen, adding the cabinets, granite countertops, and appliances. I hope you like."

"Seth, I'd be nuts not to. You've outdone yourself. This is beautiful, and I wouldn't change a thing." She wrinkled her nose, grimacing as she pointed at the ten-point buck over the fireplace. "Except, maybe that. Unless it would hurt your feelings." She shivered. "It kind of creeps me out."

I started laughing, hugging her up close. "I certainly don't want my new wife creeped-out over my prized possession. I'll hang it in my office. Will that do?"

"Ah, Seth. I'm sorry. It's just—"

"Don't be." I tweaked her nose, before giving her a light kiss and releasing her. "Are you ready for the rest of the tour?"

"Yes, please. And I promise to keep my dislikes to myself."

"Don't you dare. This is your home now. I want your honest opinions and suggestions."

All during the tour of the rest of the house and while cooking the steaks, my mind kept wandering back to Dick Smith, very likely not his name. Still, who was he?

Moving Lori into the house immediately was no longer an option. At least, not until I found out who had come calling when I wasn't here.

Chapter 20

Lori

Having dinner with Seth in my soon to be new home made me ecstatic. I wanted to move in tomorrow.

And why couldn't I? Seth had already asked me to move in, hadn't he?

We had eaten, cleaned up the kitchen, and were sitting on the leather sofa in front of a blazing fire, soft music playing in the background. His arm was draped over my shoulder. I was resting my head against his chest, loving the security of being here close to him.

"I've reconsidered your offer."

"What offer is that?" He looked down at me puzzled.

"Now that I've seen the place, and know there is little I need to do to settle in, I would like to move into our house this weekend, if it's still all right with you."

He stiffened, and then removed his arm. And like I had seen him do before when figuring out a critical problem, he leaned forward, clasped his hands together, resting his elbows on his knees.

"What's wrong? Have you changed your mind about me moving?" It hurt a little to think he'd changed his mind.

"It's not that. Like you said. It'll take a lot of your time putting the house in order, with you teaching and getting around for our wedding. It might be best if you wait until after we're married to move." He didn't look at me, just studied his hands, as if it were the most important thing to do at the moment.

"Okay. I'll wait … if you can come up with a better excuse than what you just gave me." I tapped him on the shoulder. "Look at me, Seth. I don't like talking to your back."

He turned, and with his hands on my cheeks, he leaned over gave me a sweet kiss, then let go.

Breathing out loudly, he made a grimace.

"Truth. Lori, I don't know a Dick Smith. For all I know, this guy is out for revenge. I can't let you stay here alone until I know. Since he was looking for me, he might come back and break in. I'd be leaving you vulnerable." He shook his head. "I can't do that."

Clearly agitated, he rammed a hand through his hair.

"This is the reason I didn't want to fall in love with you. The reason I didn't want to marry you now. You'll be in constant danger because of me." Closing his eyes, he breathed in heavily. "Maybe we should reconsider this whole marriage thing."

I wanted to scream and tear into Seth for his senseless logic. Instead, I took a calming breath, knowing his thoughts were only for my safety.

"Best for who, Seth? Me? Or you? Because, if it's for me, don't do me any favors."

"What do you mean?" Puzzled, he stared at me.

"I'm well aware of the dangers. In fact, you've done nothing but warn me about what will probably happen if I marry you." I touched his shoulder. "All the horror stories you can come up with won't stop me from loving you."

My heart tightened in panic. "You can walk away from me and never know true happiness because of your fear. Or you can marry me and experience the love I have for you, the children I want to give you, good Lord willing, and the life we can share together, for however long God allows. I'm willing to take that chance. But are you?"

I paused, letting my words sink into his thick skull. "So which will it be, Seth?"

Holding my breath, I wasn't sure what he would say, or if he would turn me away.

He stared at me for what seemed an eternity. On the inside, I was spent. On the outside, I tried to show him how much I loved him.

"God, help us." The prayer was wrenched from his heart as he pulled me into his arms. "I can't live without you, Lori. I love you too much."

He pulled back, his gaze roaming my face. "If you're willing, then so am I. I'll willingly take whatever time God grants us together. But my prayer is, it will be until we're both old and gray."

He sealed his words with a kiss and then pulled back smiling at me.

Gulping in a breath of air, I realized I had been holding my breath, waiting on his answer. "Promise me, you will never do this to me again."

"I promise because I can't live without you."

Hearing the doorbell, I turned to Seth. "Were you expecting anyone?"

Shaking his head, he stood and reached into the end table drawer and pulled out his revolver. Seeing Seth, gun in hand, was a little shocking. However, I schooled my reaction as if him doing so was the normal course of action.

The doorbell rang again, accompanied by loud knocking.

"Lori, please go to the bathroom. Close and lock the door, and don't come out until I tell you to."

"Seth ..."

"Please do as I say. This might be nothing. But I'd feel better if I didn't have to worry about you."

"I love you."

"I love you too, but this is probably nothing more than a neighbor calling."

For the next twenty minutes, I stood huddled by the bathroom door, praying for Seth's safety while doing my best to hear what was taking place, which was impossible.

The overwhelming desire to open the door was stopped by Seth's earlier warning to stay put.

What if he was hurt and needed my help? The thought of him just outside the door in trouble had me trembling. I couldn't hold off any longer.

Stretching out my hand for the doorknob, I drew it back when I heard footsteps and then a knock.

"It's me, Lori, open the door. You can come out now."

I threw back the door and ran into his arms, burying my face in his chest. At that moment, I fully understood just how much I loved him and how my heart would shrivel up and die if I were to ever lose him. I also realized I was petrified with fear for his safety.

After I stopped trembling, I looked up at him, touching his face, searching for any sign he'd been hurt.

"Everything's fine. It was just a marshal. He came to tell me about one of his cases."

Pushing back, more than a little perturbed, I stared up at him.

"And you couldn't have come and told me? I've been closed up in that bathroom worried sick."

I stormed past him into the entry, jerked my coat off the hanger, ready to put it on.

Seth grabbed it from me. "You're not leaving angry. And there are a couple of things we need to discuss."

"And I have papers to grade and things I need to do before school in the morning."

"Lori."

The tone of his voice had me glancing up at him then looking away. I wanted to hold on to my anger. He deserved my fury and so much more for the last twenty minutes of agony he put me through.

"I'm sorry you were worried. I didn't mean to cause you concern. However, what Dick Smith had to say was in the strictest of confidence. I thought it best if you stayed where you were." He lifted my chin, regret in his eyes. "Will you forgive me?"

I released my breath, feeling ashamed for my outburst. I couldn't be angry with him.

"Yes. But next time, will you please come tell me, so I won't be huddled up in the bathroom thinking the worst has happened to you."

"Hopefully, there won't be a next time. But if there is, I promise." He kissed me. "I love you. And thanks for following my orders without question."

"So there really was a Dick Smith?"

"Yep. I couldn't believe it either until he showed me his credentials. And sure enough, it said Dick Smith." He smiled.

"How odd."

"I thought so too. Now, as to your moving in here, if you still want to, I think that's a good idea. We'll start tomorrow night moving some of your things."

He grabbed my hand, kissing my fingers, looking deep in my eyes, his shining with love.

"But tonight, as much as I hate to, I'll take Robbie and you home." He tweaked my nose. "I'm getting used to having you around. Are you sure you don't want to push the date of our marriage up a few months? Say next week?"

"Not on your life, Cowboy. I intend on doing our wedding up right and proper." I held out my jacket. "Now take me home."

Chapter 21

Seth

"You don't say." Tim's disbelief came loud and clear over the phone.

"Afraid so. Gregg Lambert is in the witness protection program. WITSEC relocated him here over a year ago. The marshal was none to happy about us digging around and nearly blowing his cover."

"Well, how were we to know? If you hadn't been suspicious of him because of Lori, he might have stayed in hiding. Who would have known? What now?"

"We leave him be. But Lori has agreed to move into my house."

"What?"

I could hear the shock in Tim's voice.

"Get your mind out of the gutter. We're changing living quarters, is all. I'm moving into her apartment. She's moving into mine, just until we're married." The last sounded so good to my ears.

"And you're doing this why?"

Rubbing the back of my neck, I didn't want to explain everything to Tim, but knew he'd never stop asking questions until I filled him in.

"If we were suspicious of Lambert, who's to say someone else won't be. I don't want Lori around a potential problem. Best to move her now, that way, she'll be all settled in by the time we're married. And I won't have to worry about someone taking Lambert out and Lori being in the big fat middle of it all."

"Makes sense."

In the background, I could hear someone speaking to Tim.

"Ah-hold on a sec, Seth."

I doodled on a pad of paper while half listening to the muffled conversation coming over the headset.

"Hey, listen, I've got to go. Hank and I need to run down a lead. But I'll call you later."

Bummed out for sitting at home while Tim was out doing our job, I tried to sound upbeat. "Anytime."

"Remember, when you move Lori, let me know. The guys around here will be happy to help."

"Sure thing. Be safe."

"Always. Later."

I put the phone down feeling restless.

Figuring there was no better time than the present to clean out old junk and pack a few things I would need while living at Lori's, I headed for my bedroom to get busy.

My cellphone rang again. "Tim, did you find something this soon."

"Sorry, dear, but this is your mother, not Tim."

"Oh, hi, Mom. I was going to call you and ask you and dad to dinner tonight."

"Good. You won't have an excuse for not coming over then."

"Well, I was wanting to take you—"

"I've already invited your sisters. Shelly said, Zack, our little Mandy, and she were coming. And since Adam was

184

free for the evening, Whitney has accepted. I invited the Ryder's too, thinking it would be nice to have Adam's family join us. I'm not sure about Lori though. Audrey didn't know her schedule, but said she thought Lori would be able to come."

"Mom—"

"And now you will be coming too. I'm so glad."

"I-ah."

"Don't you dare make an excuse. This is the first dinner since Whitney got married and your-ah-accident. They all want to see you."

"I'll be there." How was I going to break the news to Lori? We were about to be outed tonight in front of the whole family, thanks to Mom.

"Oh, I'm so glad. We'll eat at 6:30. See you then."

Mom hung up the phone effectively cutting off anything I was about to say. She probably thought I'd back out if given half a chance.

For certain, I didn't want to ask Audrey and Jim for Lori's hand in marriage before the whole gang. However, it looked like that was how it was turning out.

Lori wouldn't be very happy about tonight, if I could get her to go over to the folks at all.

I began digging through drawers, throwing what I would need into a suitcase, and all my old stuff that wasn't worth hanging onto into trash bags.

Hours later and after a long hot shower, I dragged the last bag of trash out to the curb since pickup would be tomorrow. I had already loaded several big bags of clothes and junk for recycle into my Jeep to be dropped off at the Salvation Army.

Feeling good about what I had accomplished, I pulled on my jacket and snatched up my keys. "Come on Robbie. Let's go pick up Lori."

The dog barked and pranced around my legs, anxious to go for a ride. I was more than anxious to get this night over and done with.

Tonight, before both families and our siblings and their partners, Lori and I were going to break the news we were getting married.

I had no idea how her folks would take the news.

Most parents had high hopes of their daughter marrying a lawyer, doctor, or an executive, not a police detective. And even though Lori assured me they would be fine with my profession and me as a son-in-law, I still had my doubts.

Whether they were in favor or not, it didn't matter. I was going to marry Lori, and that was the end of the discussion.

Out front of Lori's school, I leaned against the Jeep, waiting. I received several *hello, Detective Singleton* accompanied by giggles from some of the little girls as they passed by. Apparently, our passionate kiss yesterday hadn't gone unnoticed. Lori probably had to do some explaining.

The entrance door opened and out walked Lori, her face lit up as she waved.

"Hey, Beautiful."

"Hey, yourself."

This time, instead of the kiss I wanted to give, I settled for a quick one on her lips.

"What? No passionate public display of affection." She raised her brow.

"Afraid not. The last time I did that, I got reprimanded."

"At least, you're a quick learner."

I opened the door. She climbed in and spoke to Robbie, while I went around and got in behind the wheel.

"What's with all the bags in the back? Dead bodies?"

Chuckling, I said, "Afraid not. I buried them in the backyard."

"Yuck."

"You asked for that one."

"So I did."

"The bags are filled with old stuff I'm dropping off at the Salvation Army. At least, my bedroom and bathroom have been cleaned out and they are ready for you to move in."

"Speaking of which ..."

"Don't tell me you don't want to move now." I didn't want to tell her, she was moving, regardless.

"No, I'm still moving this weekend, but dinner ..." She twisted her face up into a pretty little grimace. "Before I could call Mom and invite them out for dinner, she called me. Your folks had asked us, my mom, dad, and me, over to their house for dinner. The way it sounds, everyone will be there."

"I know."

"You knew? Why didn't you say something?"

I huffed out a breath. "Mom called me earlier this afternoon and sprung the news on me about dinner. She just wasn't sure you were coming."

"Well, I am now, apparently."

She looked out the window then back at me. I could see she was battling over to tell or not to tell everyone.

"So it looks like we'll be telling our parents in front of the whole family." She worried her lip.

"Lori, are you really that worried?"

"No-ah-yes. For goodness sakes, they don't even know we're dating, and now we're going to just blurt out we're getting married."

She was near tears. "I don't want our surprise to backfire on us."

I squeezed her cold hands trying to infuse my warmth into her. "It won't. My family will love you as much as I do. *Well*, maybe not as much as I do." He wiggled his eyebrows suggestively. "But I have no fear that they'll be happy about us getting married."

"I hope so."

We pulled up in front of her apartment. I helped Lori and Robbie out of the Jeep.

"Listen, while you're changing for dinner, I'll drop the bags off. By the time I get back, you should be ready to leave."

"All right. But first, I need this."

She leaned up, pulled my head down to hers. When our lips met nothing else mattered.

"Tell me it'll be okay." The look in her eyes still held doubt.

I kissed her like I had wanted to do earlier. This waiting to get married was going to be the death of me.

"It'll be okay." I touched her cheek. "If we get there and you don't want to say anything, let me know, and we will wait for a better time. But personally, I don't believe there will be a better time than tonight."

"I agree." She squared her shoulders. "We will tell them tonight."

"Good, because I'm not sure I could conceal the fact that I'm in love with you. One look at me, and they'll know."

"I believe you may be right." She tapped my chin. "Tonight, it is." She pulled me forward and gave me another hungry kiss. This woman knew how to clear my head of all thoughts except of her.

"I hope that will tide you over until later."

"Not hardly. It has me begging for more."

"Later, Cowboy." She sashayed off out of sight, Robbie prancing by her side, knowing full well I watched.

Being married to Lori would be a wild, crazy ride, one I was going to enjoy.

"So that's how it is, huh? The gun-toting cop and the sweet pretty schoolteacher. Who would have thought?"

Lambert's cocky innuendo and sarcasim had my blood boiling. I turned to face him, not allowing my true feelings to show. Dealing on a daily basis with men like him, I knew they were always playing an angle, always trying to get a reaction. *Well, not this time, buster.*

"Lambert. I didn't see you there."

"How could you? Lori was latched onto you like a fat cop on a donut."

I wasn't about to let the guy know he was about an inch away from me knocking his lights out.

"You can be the first to congratulate me. Lori and I are getting married."

"You don't say. Well, then, I guess congrats, if that's your sort of thing. Personally, I'd rather love 'em and leave 'em. Less complications that way, if you get my drift."

"Yeah, I get your drift, but I'd think with that attitude you'd have more problems." This guy was a piece of work. "Where are you headed?"

"A business meeting." Lambert glanced around and spotted a car at the end of the block. "See you another time."

"Sure thing."

Without being too obvious, I took my time getting into the Jeep while keeping my eyes on Lambert. He walked to the end of the block, stopped by a black Audi, bent over and talked to the people inside, then slid into the passenger's side of the car. They drove past, but with the dark tinted windows, I couldn't see inside. What I did note, the license plate number of the car.

Pulling out my cell phone, I dialed Tim's number and waited for him to answer.

189

"Hey, I was just talking about you."

I smiled. "I hope it was good."

"It was. What's up?"

"I need a favor?"

"Sure thing. Shoot."

"I have a license plate number I'd like you to run for me." I rattled off the Texas tag while starting my engine.

"Is this personal or a hunch?"

I chuckled. "Let's just say it's little of both."

"Ah. Let me guess, our man Lambert."

"You've got it. My gut tells me he's still up to no good, so I'm following my instincts on this one."

"I'll get back to you later." Tim disconnected.

After backing out, I circled the block, and then got on the freeway, still feeling uneasy about Lambert. Something, other than being in WITSEC was off with that guy, and I was going to find out what, even if the marshal had warned me to back off.

I knew, moving Lori over to the house tonight wouldn't be soon enough for me.

Chapter 22

Lori

Though I knew both sets of parents would be happy about our engagement, there was always that niggling one percent of doubt that held out, spoiling the moment.

Seth figured dinner tonight with his family, including my parents, my stepbrother, Adam and his new wife, Whitney, and would be the perfect time to let both families in on our news.

I wasn't so sure.

Would Mom and Jim approve?

Right after Seth's release from the hospital, Mom acted all gung-ho and ready to push the two of us together. But that was then, and this was now, and she hadn't said so much as a *boo* about Seth lately.

And now we weren't just dating, we were engaged, had even set the date for our wedding. Would Mom still feel the same?

It didn't matter. Mom wasn't marrying Seth. And that was all I had to say on the matter.

Though he assured me his parents would love me and be happy for us, I still couldn't rid myself of that one little percent of worry. The thought they might have someone else picked out for their son had my body trembling.

As we drove, Seth made small talk to keep me from demanding he take me back home. The drive was excruciating. When we were almost there, he pulled over to the curb and turned off the motor.

"What are you doing? Why are we stopping here?" I looked around at our surroundings.

"I was going to do this after we told everyone, but I think you need this now, more than they need to see me give it to you."

Seth pulled out a small jeweler's case. When he lifted the lid, the solitaire winked at me, causing me to tear up.

"Oh, Seth, it's beautiful." I reached for the box.

"No, let me." He pulled the ring out and held my left hand.

"Lori, will you marry me?"

"Yes, you know I will."

"I will do my utmost to make you happy so you will never regret the day we met. I love you with all my heart, soul, and body. I never thought it could be possible to love someone as much as I love you. You have made my days brighter and my nights miserable."

"Miserable?" I frowned.

"Yes, because you're not my wife yet, lying next to me in bed."

His sexy smile made me blush.

"Oh." The warmth of his words ignited a flame in my heart.

He slipped the ring on my finger and then sealed it with a kiss. "I love you beyond measure. Thank you for saying *yes*?"

"Oh, Seth, that was so lovely." I wiped my cheeks, then held up my hand to look at the ring Seth had chosen especially for me.

Even in the dusky light, the beautiful oval shaped solitaire winked and flickered up at me.

Though it was a little awkward in the Jeep, I hugged him, wishing we were anywhere but here. I wanted to celebrate properly in his arms, but it wasn't to be.

"So you really like it. We can find a—"

I put my fingers over his mouth. "Don't you dare say anything about my ring, or I'll punch your lights out, Cowboy"

My fingers felt his smile and the chuckle that rumbled out. I removed my hand and gave him a kiss. "Now can we go? I'm starving."

"Princess, I'm so glad you have your priorities in order." He gave me a quick kiss and then started the engine.

By the time we drove into the drive, all the old doubts came flooding back.

I knew this was a bad idea. Mom and Jim were already there, and so were Adam and Whitney. And, unless I missed my guess, the other car belonged to Seth's oldest sister, Shelly, and her husband, Zack Miller.

I clasped my hands in my lap, biting my lower lip. Looking at all the cars, I knew what waited for us inside.

Near tears, I gabbed Seth's sleeve, my heart nearly pounding out of my chest.

"Can we go home now?"

***

Seth

"As much as it pains me to say *no*, we can't leave. They're expecting us."

"What if our families don't like the idea of us getting married?"

"Does it really matter?" The moment I said the words, I knew it did.

I held her hand trying to bolster her courage. "Listen, they will be ecstatic. My parents will be amazed that I was able to catch someone so beautiful, intelligent, and so concerned with their feelings, not to mention, you love me."

"*Ahh*, Seth, I do love you, but I don't know about this."

I smiled. "Now me, they always said I didn't have an ounce of compassion in my bones, and that's why I became a cop."

Lori gave my cheek a loving caress. "They're wrong. You're the most sensitive man I know."

A banging on the side panel of my door had me looking out the window and then down. Mandy, my little four-year-old niece was there, waving at me to get out of the Jeep.

I motioned for her to give me a minute.

"I think it's too late to leave. They already know we are here."

Lori bit her lower lip, and then took a deep breath. "All right. I'm ready."

Before I could open the door, she pulled on my sleeve. "You better not leave me alone in there."

I leaned over and gave her a quick kiss. "I won't. I'll stick to you like tar, or glue, or whatever it is."

"I think the proper cliché is glue."

She was smiling when I opened the door to climb out.

I picked up Mandy and swung her in the air as she squealed with delight.

"Again, Uncle Seth, again."

"One more time, then we need to go inside so Lori and I can say hello to Grandma and Grandpa."

"Lori's here?" She looked around, but before she could find Lori, I swung her up in the air and around in a circle again. Mandy was giggling by the time I let her down.

"Hey, Mandy."

"Lori." Mandy wobbled-ran to Lori and gave her a hug. "Your mama and daddy are here."

"I know. I saw their car."

"My new Uncle Adam and Auntie are here, too." She looked up at me. "And you know what?"

"No. What?"

"Mommy said you're gonna be my Auntie like Auntie Witty. Uncle Seth and you are gonna get married. Can I be the flower girl?" She pounced her little hands on her waist.

"Well, I—"

"But I don't want to marry that mean ol' Brandon though."

Lori and I laughed, and then she looked at me accusingly.

I shrugged. "Hey, don't look at me. I haven't said a word."

"Why won't you say a word?" Mandy's little brow puckered up.

"Hey, you wanna see what I have in my pocket?"

My little niece started jumping up and down. "Yes! Please."

"Nice save, Mr. Slick." Lori watched as I pulled out a pink and turquoise plastic necklace and some little bracelets to match.

While Mandy became engrossed in putting the necklace and bracelets on, I leaned over and gave Lori a quick kiss.

"You see. I'll not only be a good husband, but a great dad too."

Taking her hand, we walked to the door that was already open. Mandy had run in before us to show everyone her present.

The quiver of Lori's hand let me know she was still anxious and having second thoughts about telling everyone.

Dad met us at the door. One glance at our interlocked hands, he didn't miss the diamond on her finger. Without remotely trying for subtle, he grinned watching Lori before turning to me.

"Well, I see we're too late to witness the proposal. I hope you are going to tell us when the big day will be. Or are we invited?" My father chuckled, while the whole room erupted in chaos.

"Way to go, Dad. I kind of wanted to make the announcement myself."

"We were all taking bets." He winked at Lori.

Lori looked shocked while squeezing my hand.

"Not really." Dad shook his head. "But we were all wondering if you were going to make a big announcement at dinner. Welcome to the family." He pulled Lori into a bear hug and then motioned us into the living room.

Everyone gathered around all talking at once, wanting to see Lori's ring.

Adam pulled me off to the side. "And just when were you going to let us know this was all going down?"

"Today. But Dad preempted me. You're on board, aren't you?" I wanted Lori's stepbrother to agree, but I was going to marry Lori regardless.

"I'm not so sure." Adam studied me then glanced in Lori's direction.

For the first time, I was the one squirming. It felt odd, because I'm usually the person to cause others to sweat and feel the screws being twisted up tight.

"I love her, Adam."

"You better, or you'll answer to me."

I grinned, remembering saying something similar to him just a few months back.

"Well, I guess we are to be congratulated for our Lori making an excellent choice in a partner for life." Lori's stepfather, Jim, held out his hand.

"Thank you, sir."

Lori came up beside me and slipped her arm through mine.

I regarded Audrey, Lori's mom.

"We originally didn't have plans to make a public announcement. We were going to talk with our parents first. However, since we've been preempted, I would like your permission to marry your daughter. I will do my utmost to make her happy. I love her, and if you will say yes, you'll make me the happiest man alive."

Audrey titled her head to one side, an impish twinkle in her eyes too much like her daughter's. The woman was milking the moment for all it was worth by keeping me in suspense.

Right then and there, I knew Lori was just like her mother. Together, they'd keep me on my toes.

"Would it matter one way or the other?"

"Yes, because you wouldn't only make me happy, but your daughter, also."

"Lori, why wasn't I told about Seth and you?"

"Because I knew you would become a mother-on-a mission, with your purpose in life to make sure Seth and I got married."

"She has you there, Audrey." Jim raised his brow, laughing.

"*Well*, I say *yes*." Audrey gave me a hug. "Welcome to the family." She tipped her face up and planted a kiss on my cheek.

My two sisters joined us.

"I told you they would make a perfect couple." Whitney was speaking to Shelly. "And I was right."

Whitney gave me a sly grin. "You didn't fool anyone with your teasing and picking on Lori. I knew the way you watched her, you were falling hard, and it would be just a matter of time."

"Good job, brother. Welcome to this nutty family, Lori." Shelly gave her a hug.

"Thanks. I got the best part of the bargain." I hugged Lori up tight. "Let me tell you, it was touch and go there for a while. I wasn't sure I would be able to convince her. Fortunately, she came around and finally said yes."

"I wasn't sure if he was teasing or serious. But I decided I'd give him the benefit of a doubt and marry him to keep him out of trouble."

"Good luck with that one. Where my son goes, trouble's bound to follow."

"Thanks, Dad. Don't do me any favors. Can't you at least wait to tell her my bad side until after we've tied the knot? I don't want her running off."

"Why, Sugar, you just let your Daddy talk. I want to hear all about your little misadventures so I'll know what I'm up against."

Everyone began laughing.

I wasn't sure if it was Lori's southern drawl that caused their reaction, or my family thinking up all the juicy tales to entertain Lori while watching me squirm.

"Well, when are you going to introduce your intended to me, you scallywag?" Grams rocked while a steady stream of crocheted yarn produced an intricate pattern from her hook.

Up until this moment, she'd sat silently listening to everyone talk. It appeared she was ready to put her two cents' worth in the pot.

"We're coming now, Grams." I led Lori over to my grandmother, not knowing what to expect.

"Grams, this is Lori Morgan, my fiancée. You met her at Whitney's wedding. She's Adam's sister."

"Certainly, I remember her."

"Mrs. Bachman, so nice to see you again." Lori shook Grams' hand.

"So, you're the one who's captured my grandson's heart."

"Yes, ma'am, it seems I have."

"Good, cause it will take a good, strong woman to keep up with Seth."

"I believe I'm up to the task." Lori glanced up at me. "If not, do I have your permissions to send him over to you so you can get him back in line."

Grams cackled. "I like your girl, Seth. I can tell she's not going to take any sass off of you."

"I believe you're right."

Grams' eyes sparkled. "If you really want to know about Seth, you just ask me. I've got a trunk full of tales. "

"Gram's, you don't want to scare Lori off, do you? Especially, since you've been after me forever to find a wife and settle down."

"You might be right about that. But once you're married, I'll give her the full lowdown."

"Thank you, Mrs. Bachman. I look forward to hearing your tales."

"It's Grams. All the family calls me Grams."

Lori beamed. "Thank you, Grams."

"Lori, you remember my Aunt Polly."

"Yes I do. Polly, so nice to see you again."

"I can't tell you how happy I am for the both of you." Aunt Polly dabbed her eyes. "Mama and I have been praying ever so long for just the right girl to come along for our Seth. And here you are." Aunt Polly gave Lori a hug.

"Seth, here, won't tell you, but a lot of women have been after him for years. Mind you, he wouldn't take a second look. So I know you've got to be someone special for him to break his own imposed rule not to marry."

Lori pulled her arm through mine. "He tried to get me to wait for five long years, but I didn't agree. So we compromised. Four months."

She leaned in close to my aunt and grandmother.

"You won't believe what he wanted to do after we set the date."

"Knowing Seth like we do, I can just about imagine."

"Lori." My warning went unheeded.

"He wanted to push the date up, but of course, I told him *no*."

Grams laughed again. "That sounds like our Seth. When he wants something, he doesn't care to wait."

By now everyone was seated around the room listening.

"Have you set a date yet?" This came from Mom, who, like the rest of the group, had been listening to Grams' and Aunt Polly's exchange with Lori.

I pulled Lori up tight against me. "June first is what Lori says. But if I have my way, it will be next week."

The rest of the room erupted into *no, you can't do that*, and *don't you dare*, along with other such words, all coming from the women in the room.

All the men had another opinion, which pretty well matched mine. *The sooner, the better.*

Chapter 23

Lori

To say I was exhausted was putting it mildly. I enjoyed myself at the family dinner. Still, my nerves were frayed even though everyone had accepted the fact Seth and I were getting married.

After dinner, all the women dragged me off to the kitchen. We talked about wedding plans and everything else connected with what it would take to get one ready in less than four months.

The streetlights streamed across the plains of Seth's handsome face. I could see the strain of the evening had taken a toll on him also.

"Listen, though I've packed some things like you asked me to do, I'm so tired, I'd rather stay in my apartment tonight. You can come over early in the morning when I'm fresh. We can move my things then."

Seth's frown told me he didn't like my idea.

"What difference will one night make?"

"I have an alarm system in place. You don't. I'd just feel better if you would stay at our house tonight."

"*Seth* ..." My little whine of his name didn't move him in the least.

He reached for my hand.

"Honey, please, humor me. We'll pick up your suitcase. I'll take you to the house. I'll leave, and you can go straight to bed. When you're awake in the morning, you can call me. I'll come pick you up and move the rest of your things, or at least as much as we can tomorrow."

"I wish I knew what you aren't saying. Am I in some kind of danger? Are you in danger?" I watched for his reaction and noticed a slight twitch in his jaw.

"No, neither of us. What makes you think that?"

"The way you're acting and doing your best to keep me from staying at my place, is what."

He lifted my hand and kissed the back. "If you were in danger—"

"You wouldn't tell, would you?"

"That depends. If it were an imminent threat, I'd warn you to be watchful."

"Yeah, and have a 24-hour guard stationed outside my door." I mumbled, watching him closely. "Is this what I can expect will happen as a detective's wife?"

"Partially." He gave a funny little grimace. "I'm going to tell you something I shouldn't, and I'm trusting you to keep this in the strictest of confidence. No one is to know."

"Seth, anything you tell me will always be safe. Now, what is it you didn't want to say?"

"You're neighbor, Gregg Lambert?"

"Yes." I had a feeling I wasn't going to like what he was about to say.

"He's in witness protection."

"You've got to be kidding." The thoughts of someone notorious living down the hall from me had me a little uneasy. "And here I thought Gregg was a friendly sort of guy. I would have never guessed."

"Not only that, I think whatever got him into WITSEC, he's dabbling in it again. My suspicions and his interest in you are the reasons I want you to stay at our house from here on out. If he's up to no good, which I believe he is, then you'll be safe and out of his reach."

"Why would he want to harm me? I've been nothing but kind to the man."

"He probably doesn't want to harm you. But since you're acquainted, if he feels any threat to his safety, he could become violent. Or the people he's dealing with may use you thinking to get to him. I don't want to take that chance."

"I understand. I'll stay at the house. But you be careful."

He grinned, quite pleased he'd won this argument. "Always."

By the time I was finally settled in at Seth's house, and he'd left for my apartment, my mind wouldn't calm down. Thankfully, I didn't have school tomorrow. If I had, I would've been dead on my feet.

Propped up in bed, my computer on my lap, I began doing research for our wedding. I made up a spreadsheet of all the different places and prices. This whole wedding thing was turning out to be a huge expense. I wasn't sure it was a good outlay of cash. But, a wedding there was going to be. Just how big was yet to be determined.

My eyes finally started to droop, and I set my computer on the nightstand. I snuggled deep beneath the covers, determined to ask Seth if he wanted a big wedding with all the expense, or would he be disappointed if it was only close family and friends.

A nice, long honeymoon, just the two of us alone, would be enjoyable though.

***

I rolled over, yanked the covers up over my ears, ignoring the noise. The obnoxious sound of my cellphone wouldn't stop. Snatching it off the nightstand, I saw it was Seth and smiled.

Clearing my throat, I said, "Hi, Cowboy."

"Hey, sleepyhead, don't tell me you aren't up yet."

"Okay, I won't."

His deep throaty chuckle caused delicious feelings to run through me. "I was going to ask how you slept last night, but I don't think I need to."

"What time is it?" I stretched my legs, feeling the pull of my taut muscles, while loving the feel of the soft warm bed.

"Eleven."

"Eleven?" I jerked upright into a sitting position, shoving the hair from my face. "You've got to be kidding. Why didn't you call me earlier? I have too much to do to be lying around in bed."

"We're all primed and ready to move your stuff into the house." He chuckled. "I've got donuts and sausage rolls waiting for you, so get up and get dressed."

"How long will it be before you're here?" I heard a thumping and Robbie's nails clacking on the tile floor as he ran to the front door barking.

"I'm here now, outside waiting on you. Get a move on it sleepy head, or we'll have to eat these without you."

"I'm moving, I'm moving." I threw the covers back.

"Before you start getting dressed, could you take the bar off the door so I can come in and make coffee?"

"Yeah, sure. Give me just a minute." I swung my legs off the bed.

"Oh, by the way, Tim's here with me."

"Hi, Lori." Tim was yelling in the background.

"I'm hanging up now." Embarrassed at being caught in bed at this hour, I scrambled for my robe. I ran my fingers through my hair, not wanting Seth or Tim see me looking like a scarecrow. I hurried to the front and unbolted the door. "Give me thirty seconds and then come in."

"One thousand one, one thousand two …"

"Ha-ha, very funny." I made a mad dash back to the bedroom.

By the time I was decent, my hair combed and in a ponytail, and a smidgeon of makeup on, I followed my nose to the kitchen. The coffee was brewed. Three plates and two cups were sitting on the counter. Tim was sitting up at the bar sipping from his cup. Seth was nowhere in sight.

He came up behind me, slipped his arms around my waist. "*Mmm*, you smell good enough to eat." He nibbled my neck.

"Get a room." Tim rolled his eyes.

"We will in June, but until then …" He turned me around and gave me one good kiss that tingled all the way down to my toes. He released me. "Mornin', Princess."

"Good morning." My cheeks flamed, knowing we had an audience.

He didn't seem to be affected one iota.

I looked around. "Did you happen to feed Robbie?"

"Sure did."

"Thanks. Now where are those sausage rolls?"

Tim laughed. "You sure know how to pick 'em, Seth. Your gal has the right priorities, food first, then work."

Ignoring Tim, I grabbed one of the rolls Seth held out to me. They smelled delicious. I closed my eyes, taking the first bite of food since last night. My mouth watered as my teeth clamped down into the sweet, salty goodness.

"*Mmm*. These are so good."

"Yup, you know how to pick 'em. She can make a real production of just eating a sausage roll."

I wadded up my napkin and threw it at Tim's head. He didn't see it coming. It hit him square between the eyes.

"And she's a sure-shot too." Tim laughed. "Yup. This one's a keeper.

Giving him the evil eye, I said, "If you're not careful, you're very apt to have a flying saucer hit you next."

"Yikes, I won't say *no* more."

"For once, you've made a wise choice." I nodded.

"How was the first night in your new home? Think you're going like it here?" Seth took a bite of his donut, watching me.

"No thinking about it. I love my new home, and I slept very well, thank you."

"Good." Seth polished off his donut, took the last swig of coffee, and then rinsed his cup in the sink before putting it in the dishwasher.

"And he's domesticated too. You didn't ask me how I slept, Seth, dear." Tim apparently woke up feeling great by the way he was clowning around.

Thinking to turn the tables on him, I asked, "How's Connie, Tim?" I realized I'd asked the wrong thing when he looked down into his cup, frowning and shrugged.

"Okay, I guess."

"Oh. I see." I polished off another sausage roll and drank the last sip of my coffee. Brushing my hands together, I said, "Well, I've been fed, and now I'm ready to do some work. Shall we go, guys?"

Robbie danced around my feet, anxious to go too.

"Not this time, fella. You have to stay and guard the house. We'll be back in a little bit. Now go to your room."

Robbie slowly made his way, taking several sad glances back at us.

I reached into his doggie treats, slipped him a biscuit, then gave him a good couple of rubs.

"When we're through moving, I'll take you for a walk in the neighborhood so you can meet your new neighbors. How does that sound?"

Robbie barked.

I sauntered back into the kitchen and hooked my arm in Tim's.

Seth looked at me strange-like.

"Now, would you like to tell me what's going on with Connie?"

"That's just it. Nothing."

We walked out the door, heading to the car, leaving Seth to set the alarm and lock up the house.

"We've gone out on a couple of dates, but she didn't seem all that excited."

"She may be afraid you're not serious. That you're just looking at her as someone to pass the time with and nothing more?" I climbed in the back and strapped in, allowing Tim to ride shotgun.

"My advice, and you can take it or leave it, mind you, would be to call her again and ask her for another date. That way she'll know you're serious, or at least, she'll begin to think you are. Only this time, take her flowers, dine at a nice restaurant, and, after all that, take her to see the latest and greatest chick-flick."

I smiled, wiggling my eyebrows. "Nothing says *I love you* like a man sitting through a tear-jerker romance. If she doesn't act interested after that, then I'd say, forget her and move on."

I winked at Seth as he looked in the rearview mirror to back out of the drive.

"You deserve someone as nice as your friend here found."

Tim wrinkled his nose looking at Seth trying to understand what I meant.

"Ah, but you'll never be able to find someone as nice as I found." Seth winked at me. "They didn't just break the mold when they made Lori, they broke the machine, too."

"Why, thank you, sweet pea."

He must have seen my smirk from the review mirror.

"Hold on to your boots, Tim. She's about to give us a bucket load."

"Why whatever do you mean, Sugar Pie?" Pouring on a thick southern drawl, I could hardly keep a straight face.

"Let me tell you something about your friend here, Tim. It's like this. It's true Seth and I had a rocky beginning. No one knows the agonies I suffered." I clutched my heart giving him a *poor-me* face.

"I figured this man would be the death of me with all his picking and sniping. I'm sure those who watched us believed ours was a match made in … well, you know, that other place. Certainly not heaven." I smacked my lips, looking prim and proper.

"Seth here, fought like a tiger with every fiber of his being to resist my womanly charms. But let me tell yah, he was no match for my animal magnetism." I growled like a cheetah, clawing at the air with my fingers.

"Now listen up, Tim. I want you to believe me when I say … I don't plan on letting a day go by after we've said *I do*, that I don't remind your friend here that he fought tooth and hangnail to keep from loving me."

I thought about breaking out in song, but was afraid Seth might have a wreck. Instead, I called upon my orator's voice striking my index finger in the air.

"There isn't a mountain too tall, or a valley so low, nor running shoes fast enough to keep him from falling in love with me."

"Lori—"

"Don't interrupt. This is my story. You can tell yours another time."

He rolled his eyes at me. "You're impossible."

"You see, that's what I have to put up with, and all because I love him. However, when it came right down to the nitty-gritty of seeing who loved who, I wasn't afraid to admit my love. No, siree, Tim!

"Let me tell you, there were more times than I have fingers and toes, that I wanted to crown him over the head with my cast iron fryin' pan for being such a ninny. I nearly did too, when he asked me to wait five years to get married."

"You actually asked Lori to wait?" Tim's face was a study in disbelief.

"I—"

"Now, Honey Pie, don't you be interrupting. This here is my tale." I folded my arms over my chest. "*Humph!* When he said five years, let me tell you, I was having none of that. It was either now or never." I stopped to look out in space. "Isn't there a song that says that very thing? If there isn't, there sure should be."

I wiggled my fingers in front of Tim's face. My solitaire sparkled like a beacon on a dark moonless night.

"Seth here,"—I reached up and patted Seth on the shoulder—"will be putting another ring on my finger in June. And that, my friend, is how it is done the Lori Morgan way. Persistence, I tell you. Persistence wins the day, and ... refusing to take no for an answer."

I changed my voice to my teacher's voice. "So get to it. Be tenacious. Go capture Connie's heart."

I pasted a sugar-sweet grin on my face staring at Tim.

"But if you don't mind, would you please wait until you've helped us move my things into the house. Seth here doesn't know it, but we're gonna need all the help we can get." I sat back, enjoying the ride. "Wait till you see all the stuff I have in my closets. Seth, the poor fellow doesn't know what he's up against."

"Lori, you aren't a pack-rat, are you?" Seth sounded worried.

When I didn't answer and began humming, he appeared frazzled.

"Oh, great. I'm marrying a hoarder."

"I resemble that remark, Sweetie Pie." I chuckled. "They don't call me little Lori stockpile for nothing."

Chapter 24

Seth

We had taken the last load, at least for today, to the house. Lori stayed to clean up and get dressed, while I went back to her almost empty apartment to shower, get dressed, and then pick her up for dinner.

Knowing Lori was expecting me, I let myself in the house and walked into the living room all smiles, but on the inside I was a basket case. I wanted to make sweet memories for Lori to remember when we were old and gray. And I knew I had fallen short in that department.

It amazed me that someone so lovely and sweet could actually love me. And like now, Lori dressed for our date, sitting on the sofa, and smiling up at me. My love grew in intensity until it felt like my heart would burst.

Closing her computer, she slid it onto the coffee table. "Hey, you."

"Hey back at'cha." I was overwhelmed by emotions.

She stared at me oddly. "What'cha got behind your back?"

I pulled out a huge bouquet I had gotten from the florist and held it in front of her. "These are for you."

She jumped up from the couch and into my arms, giving me a warm, welcoming kiss. The kiss was hot, passionate, and sweet, all rolled into one.

Taking the flowers from my hands, she buried her nose in them, taking a deep breath.

"They're beautiful, Seth, and they smell so good. Thank you." She kissed me on the cheek, then walked into the kitchen. "Do you have a vase?"

"Nope, afraid not. I should have thought to buy one."

"No worries. I saw a pitcher here somewhere." She opened a few cupboard doors. "Here it is."

After filling the glass pitcher with water, she put the flowers in, fluffed them up a little and then moved them to the kitchen bar. She stood back smiling. "There. Aren't they beautiful."

"I wasn't deaf."

"Deaf?" She looked mystified. "What do you mean?"

"I heard what you told Tim in the Jeep this morning about wining and dining his gal. That's when I realized it was something I hadn't done. I'm sorry."

Worry filled her face. "Oh, I hope you didn't think I was saying all that for your benefit."

"No, but it got me to thinking. Ours hasn't been a conventional courtship. We had a different kind. I never gave you flowers, took you to fancy restaurants, or gave you gifts, or sat through a chick-flick. So I figured I'd start tonight. I want you to have lovely memories before and after we're married."

She touched my cheek. "I do. All my memories are sweet, funny, and they're all about you."

I pulled out my next gift. "Name the date and time, and I'll watch this with you. I've got to see who this Darcy guy is."

"Oh, Seth." Tears gathered in her eyes as she looked at the movie, *Pride and Prejudice*. It's one of my favorite stories. Thank you."

I knew it was corny, but I knelt on one knee and took her hand.

"Lori, I will do my best to make you happy so you will never regret marrying me. I thank God everyday that you walked into my life. I will always love and cherish you."

I stood and wrapped my arms around her, but not before I saw her mischievous glint.

"Well, aren't you supposed to kiss me or something? I've been waiting ever so long for—"

I captured her soft lips with mine, deepening the kiss, wanting more of her, but knew I would have to wait until we said *I do*.

When I broke the kiss, I rested my forehead on hers.

"Are you sure you don't want to move our wedding date up? Just being in the same room with you drives me crazy."

"Hmm, after that kiss, you might have a point. That one positively knocked my socks off." She looked down at her bare wiggling toes. "See, there's your proof."

"You didn't have any socks on in the first place."

"Well, that may be true. But if I'd had socks on, your kiss would have blown them right off my feet.

Latching my arms around her tightly, I picked her up and swung her around.

"Put me down, silly, you're making me dizzy."

"I want you dizzy with love so that you will change our wedding date." I swung her around one more time and then put her down.

"We can't Seth. What about our honeymoon? I can't leave before school lets out. And our parents and family are expecting to be a part of our wedding. No matter how hard it is on both of us, we'll have to wait till June first."

213

"You want to know something?"

"What?"

"I'll wait"—I tweaked her nose—"but I won't like it."

She tipped up on her toes, gave me a kiss that nearly knocked my socks off, and I *was* wearing some.

"I won't like it either, Seth. But we'll manage."

Holding up her hand, she wiggled her fingers, looking at her engagement ring.

"Oh, Seth, my ring is so beautiful. I can't wait to show it to my friends tomorrow."

She frowned. "Oh, no! Now look what you've gone and done." Again she wiggled her fingers.

Since I didn't have a clue what she was talking about, I got a little worried. "What did I do?"

"You've given me this gorgeous ring, and just look at my nails."

I looked but didn't see anything. "What's wrong with your nails?"

"Men! They never see what's right under their nose. Why should I have thought you'd be any different?" She rolled her eyes. "I need a manicure, is what. I can't show off my ring tomorrow at church with my nails looking like I've been clawing my way to China. I wonder if one of the places in the mall is still open?"

Laughing, I said, "That's what I love about you, your zaniness. Don't ever change."

"Oh, believe me, what you see is what you get." She gave me a sassy smile.

"Go on." I pushed her toward the entry. Get your coat. I'll put Robbie up, and then I'll drive you to the mall to see if you can find a place for a manicure. Then we'll have dinner to celebrate your new nails." I waited to see what she'd say.

"Nails aren't something you celebrate." She pursed her lips, frowning. "But our engagement?" She raised her brows, grinning. "Now that's worth celebrating."

***

Lori

Since it was seven o'clock when the woman finished my nails, Seth drove us to a quaint little restaurant on Greenville Avenue. The place reminded me of one of those little romantic European restaurants you see in the ads.

We sat at a corner table by the window with a view of the street. Couples, hand in hand, strolled by as cars drove slowly down the street.

"See." I held out my hand for the umpteenth time, wiggling my fingers to make the diamonds sparkle in the light. "My nails almost look worthy of my ring. Now I'm ready to show the world and let them know I'm marrying Seth Singleton."

He reached across the table and took hold of my hand. "Are you sure you don't have any regrets?"

"If you don't stop talking like that, I'll come over there and give you some regrets."

I gave him an *I dare you* glare. "Better yet, I'll kiss you until you say *uncle,* or they throw us out of this place. So which will it be?"

"I'll stop. But I want you to be sure."

"I'm sure. Otherwise, I would have said *no* when you proposed."

A couple of tables away, a man who must have had too much to drink started yelling at his wife, drawing our attention.

The poor woman ducked her head, wiping her face. The manager went to their table, said a few words. The man got angrier and began threatening the manager.

The poor man looked around for help, but all the wait staff had mysteriously disappeared.

Seth released my hand. "I'm sorry, but I think I'd better see if I can help calm the man down. Otherwise, things are going to get messy."

I nodded, feeling a knot of fear tighten in my stomach.

When Seth approached the scene, the bully turned on Seth, using a few choice words about him keeping his nose out of where it didn't belong.

As I watched, twisting my hands, I prayed for his safety, my emotions running high. I saw firsthand what Seth had tried to tell me about his job being dangerous.

The man tried to take a swing at him, which Seth deflected. Instead, the man ended with his arm up behind his back in a vice grip instead. Though I couldn't hear what was said, except for what the man yelled, I was proud my guy had everything under control.

Seth got up close to the man's ear and said something to him. Immediately, the man turned meek and mild. I wanted to stand and applaud and tell everyone that's the guy I'm going to marry. Instead, I held my seat and beamed.

"I believe these people would like their food to go and to pay their bill." Seth spoke to the manager.

The bully started to protest. But Seth gave him a look that closed the man's mouth, causing him to lowered his head, nodding.

Within seconds, the couple's food was in boxes and sacked, the bill paid, and Seth was walking the man out the door, the woman following.

Seth came back in and sat down across from me he acted as if he'd done nothing more than go to the men's room.

I smiled and said, "I can't take you anywhere without you showing out, can I?"

"Sorry about that." He looked sheepish

"Seth, don't apologize. I was teasing. You were amazing."

He wrinkled his brow. "Hardly."

"Listen, if I say you're amazing, then you are amazing. I was so proud of how you handled that man. Anyone else, and I believe there would have be a brawl in the restaurant."

Seth glowed with my compliment, but refused to acknowledge he had a hand in settling a public disturbance.

The waiter walked up with our tea and salads. He looked at Seth like he was some kind of hero. And he was. Mine.

I cleared my throat, and cocked my one brow as if to say, *see, I'm not the only who thinks you're awesome.*

Seth chuckled, shaking his head.

Fortunately, the rest of our meal went along flawless and without any more drama. Each course was delicious, even the dessert that we didn't order but miraculously appeared, fabulous.

When Seth asked for the ticket, the manager came to our table.

"Detective Singleton, if you had not chosen my establishment to eat, I hate to think what would have happened. I owe you my gratitude. I hope you will be a repeat customer. However, your dinner has been taken care of."

Seth shook his head. "No, I can't let you pay for it."

"Oh, you mistake my meaning. The wife of the gentleman you helped-ah-escort out to their car, called. She paid by credit card, and said to make sure you and your lovely companion received dessert for all you did to keep her-ah-husband from landing in jail."

"Thank you."

The manager smiled at me and then at Seth. "Have a good evening, and I hope you will come again."

"We will. The food was delicious." Seth looked at me. "Shall we go?"

We walked to the car and once inside, I asked, "Seeing you in action ... *wow* ... words don't adequately express how well you handled the situation. Our dinner could have turned out to be a fiasco. Instead, you offered entertainment too."

"I'm glad I could accommodate." He crinkled his brow, more put out with me than happy.

"Seth, what you did was enlightening, and something I wouldn't have missed for all the tea in Brooklyn."

"I believe that's China." He chuckled.

"You say it your way, I'll say it mine." I stuck my nose in the air, then smile. "No, really, you have a knack for handling people."

"Except when it comes to you."

"Hmm. You can handle me anytime." I gave him an impertinent smile.

"If I wasn't driving this car, I'd kiss you silly?"

"May I suggest you pull over into that driveway up ahead?"

"And what, attract another cop to tell me this isn't Lover's Lane. No thank you, I'll wait."

"Ah, shucks."

The happenings of earlier triggered my memory. "Hey, did you ever follow up with the little boy with the broken arm."

At first, he gave me a puzzled glance, and then his face cleared. "Yeah, I did."

"What happened?"

"It was as I suspected. The father is abusive. The family court allowed the mother to keep the boy as long as the father didn't have any contact. Once he's through with his anger management counseling and he's proved he can hold onto his temper, he'll get to visit with supervision."

He took a deep breath then released it. "I hope he can get his act together. Otherwise, the boy will grow up without his father. But if living without abuse means no father, then the boy is better off."

"I'm so glad you were able to help the mother and the boy."

He brushed my compliment aside.

When Seth pulled in the drive, he came around, helped me out and walked me to the door. He pulled me into his arms, drew me close, breathing in my scent.

"Lori, I didn't believe it was possible, but I love you more with each passing moment."

He captured my lips, sending my emotions careening all over the place. When he broke our kiss, I wanted to beg him for more. Seeing his eyes heavy with desire, I knew Seth was at his limits.

I leaned my head against his chest, and he rested his head on top of mine. We stood that way until I noticed his heart and mine were beginning to settle back to almost normal.

His arms fell away, and I felt cold and lonely.

"I'll pick you up in the morning for church."

"Okay.

"Would you like me to bring you breakfast?"

"If you keep bringing me donuts and sausage rolls, I'm going to turn into a porker."

"I'll love you whatever you look like."

"Be that as it may, I don't want to waddle down the aisle to say my vows."

219

"All right. I won't bring breakfast." He gave me another kiss, which was barely romantic. He opened the door, stepped in to turn off the alarm then turned and walked outside. "I'll see you in the morning."

"And I'll wear bells on my toes and a diamond on my finger." I wiggled my fingers at him.

"Leave the bells at home, please. Love you. Now go inside, lock the door, and set the alarm."

"Aye, aye, my captain."

I shut the door, then leaned against it, the chill seeping through my coat.

"Lori. I'm not leaving."

Chuckling, I said, "Oh. All right." I turned the bolt. "How's that?"

"And don't forget the alarm."

I stuck out my tongue, knowing he couldn't see me, then smiled, and said saucily. "*Yes, mother.*"

That guy could be so infuriating, but I loved every inch of him and couldn't wait to marry the man.

Chapter 25

Lori

Like Dallas pre-summer days can be, it was warm and sunny. Any later in the year and our wedding reception outside by my folk's pool would have been miserable.

The wedding itself was a blur in my mind. All I remember is walking down the aisle, my arm hooked in Jim's. With every step, he patted my arm doing his best to calm my nerves, telling me what a fine young man I was marrying, to which I agreed.

When I saw Seth, standing up front looking so handsome in his black tux next to Pastor Steve, I wanted to run up the aisle and get our vows over and done. We had waited long enough to be husband and wife.

It was four long excruciating months of challenges and frustrations to stay celibate, so that we could honor our vows to one another and God.

I barely remember saying my vows, or even hearing Seth say his. However, I remember our kiss, a kiss that will stand out in my mind till I'm old and gray. There was something different in our first married kiss. The kiss said we were truly one and now complete.

I looked over at my husband of only an hour, standing talking to Tim and Connie, who had become engaged a little over a month ago.

Seth was laughing. The sound made my heart do flip-flops. Knowing this magnificent specimen of a man belonged to me still didn't seem real.

Thank God, I had seen through the smokescreen Seth had erected to keep me at arms lengths. If I hadn't, I would have missed out on all Seth's love.

It still bothered me some, knowing he would always be in danger, something I would never let him know. He worried enough about me without me adding my worries to his plate.

A day living with my gentle giant was worth any amount of worry that plagued me while he was on the job.

Aware that Seth had come up behind me, I leaned into him as his arms surrounded my waist. His cheek rested against mine.

"What if it hadn't been me behind you?"

"Ah, but I knew it was you. My body is fine-tuned to yours. I get a certain vibe when you are even remotely close to me."

"Is that so?" He squeezed me tight up against him.

"Uh-huh." I leaned my head back against his chest, wishing we were already on our honeymoon.

"Happy?" He kissed my cheek and then moved to capture my ear, sending chills to cascade through my whole body.

"No." I teased.

He growled. "Then I'll keep this up until you are."

I chuckled. "Ecstatic is the word that comes to mind. Today, Mr. Singleton, I married the man of my dreams. I have waited my whole life for this day, and now it's almost gone."

I turned my head, craning my neck to look up at my husband. "How about you? Are you happy?"

"There aren't words enough to describe how I feel, but I'm willing to show you."

I glanced back to where our friends and family stood talking and laughing while I, nestled in Seth's arms, was surrounded by love.

"What do you say about getting this show over so we can get on down the road?"

Smiling, I said, "I thought you would never ask. But since you have, I say yes, lead on, oh, husband, mine."

His arms fell away. He grabbed my hand, practically dragging me across the lawn to the table that held our wedding cake.

"I believe there's a cake to cut, toasts to be made before we can respectfully say our goodbyes." He winked at me. "I for one, Mrs. Singleton, don't want to waste one more minute. I want you to be mine in every sense of the word."

"Why, Husband, I do declare, you have shocked my senses to the very core."

"I'll do more than shock your senses, *Sugar*, if we can ever get out of here. I'll captivate and stroke the fires of your heart till you are so consumed by my love, you'll cry *enough*."

"Never. I'll take all the love you can dish out and then beg for more. I want to grow old by your side, but I will take whatever days God allows."

I smiled up at him, hoping he knew how much I loved him. How I yearned to do whatever it would take to make him happy.

"Know this, Lori, I love you today with all my heart, mind, and soul, and that love will only grow in intensity."

"I love you back, and always will. So clink that glass and let's get this show on the road. Like you, I don't want to waste another minute. I want to begin our honeymoon and the rest of our life together."

"Here! Here!"

"Such love has no fear, because perfect love expels all fear."
I John 4:18 NLT

Other Books By Janice Olson

<u>Romantic Suspense</u>:
   "The Texas Sorority Sisters" Series ~ Romantic Suspense
       Serenity's Deception
       Lethal Intent
       Chameleon
       Run ... You Can't Hide

Romance:
   Texas Serendipity Series ~ Romance with a twist of humor:
       Mr. What's-His-Name
       Wanted a Man For Christmas

November 2016 ~ A new five book series
   The McCaslands of Primrose Texas
   Book 1 ~ **Love by the Bushel** – Garrett McCasland

Airtight Case For Love

First edition published 2015 ©
Lyndon Publishing

You may write Janice at:

P.O. Box 382380
Duncanville, Texas 75116

or by email: Janice at Janice Olson dot com

And please sign up for Janice's Newsletter and Book updates at: www.JaniceOlson.com